Nicholas Perry had gone a long way towards making Cathy trust men again. But she couldn't quite keep the niggling doubts at bay. Just why had he been so kind to her? Just because she loved him, didn't mean he loved her!

WALK INTO TOMORROW

BY

ROSEMARY CARTER

MILLS & BOON LIMITED
15–16 BROOK'S MEWS
LONDON W1A 1DR

CHAPTER ONE

'Sure now, Cathy?' Larry shouted over the noise of the helicopter.

'Quite sure.'

'It's lonely down there, girl. Cold and white and lonely.'

Cathy Lennox peered through her window at the mountains of the Canadian Rockies, all of them snow-covered. The clumps of evergreens made the only note of colour against the pristine snow.

Green eyes sparkling, she turned to the pilot. 'It's what I want.'

Wasted, was the word that came to Larry's mind. The girl was beautiful. The hood of her parka covered her head and much of her face, but he'd seen her earlier, before she'd put on all the heavy outer gear, and he'd thought her quite beautiful. Hair the colour of liquid honey, and eyes that were green and widely spaced, and a mouth that tilted deliciously at the corners when she smiled. What in heck did she think she was doing?

'Not even a phone to keep you in touch with the world.'

I don't want to be in touch with the world, Cathy thought. But she just smiled. 'That's fine. Don't worry about me, Larry.'

'I'll have to drop your stuff in the snow.'

'I know.'

'Be dark soon.' He was frowning. 'Damn shame I

couldn't get you here earlier, and of course yesterday was no go in the end ... Well, there it is.'

'I'll be just fine,' she reassured him, touched by his concern.

'Yeah, well ... How come you decided to buy the teahouse anyway?'

'Seemed like a good idea,' she said lightly, and hoped he would leave it at that.

'Listen, if you run into problems, there's always Nicholas. You've met Nick? Nicholas Perry? Owner of Turquoise Lake Hotel?'

'No.'

'You will. Good man, Nick. Get to know him, Cathy.'

'Stop worrying about me, Larry.' Her smile concealed her bitterness. She had no intention of getting to know Nicholas Perry. Nor any other man for that matter. Her sole purpose in buying the teahouse had been to get away from men.

'I'll get to know him,' she lied.

The helicopter made a turn. Larry was peering down into the snowy landscape, his furrowed face a study in concentration. At length he said, 'You can't see the place, but it's there, between those trees. Can't risk getting you down any closer than this.'

Excitement was building inside her. 'Yes!'

'Get your stuff into the cabin quickly. Be dark soon.'

'I'll be quick,' she promised.

He looked at her. 'Last chance to change your mind, girl.'

She threw him another smile. 'No way. Thanks for everything, Larry. And don't worry about me. Please. I'll be just fine.'

* * *

She watched as the helicopter became a speck in the sky, then vanished altogether. On the snow lay her possessions, her suitcases, and all the boxes of supplies. She turned her eyes to the trees. Somewhere in there was the teahouse. Larry was right, it was time to get moving. This was unfamiliar territory, and she would be wise to have all her things in the cabin before dark.

But strangely she was in no real hurry. She took a few deep breaths, loving the chill freshness of the air. All around her were mountains, tall and mysterious and covered with snow. In just a few weeks the snow would melt, and when the trails dried there would be hikers and backpackers, and some of them would find their way to the teahouse.

Only the high peaks would remain white. Ah, but it would be beautiful. She remembered how beautiful she had thought it that first time. Now it would be hers, to enjoy every day, for she knew she would never grow tired of it. Impulsively she bent, scooped up some snow, patted it into a ball and threw it across the slope. At the same time she laughed, a lovely laugh, high and joyful in the silence. She had not laughed like that for four months.

It was just four months since her world had crumbled. Four months since the attempted assault and the trial that followed it. Who would have thought then that she'd have the chance to buy the teahouse? But she *had* bought it, and she was here now. A new life was beginning for her. She'd have all the space and time to make that life just the way she wanted it.

Starting now. She tore her eyes from the mountains and looked at all her things lying in the snow. Larry would have a fit if he knew she was still standing here admiring the view. Time to make her way to the teahouse. It would take quite a while to bring everything inside. But first she wanted to see the place.

Leaving everything in the snow, she made her way towards the trees. And there it was. The log cabin nestled in the pine trees, just as she remembered it. And belonging to her. She took off a mitten so that she could take the key out of the pocket of her parka.

Suddenly she saw the smoke rising from the chimney. Smoke! And was that a light shining in the window? It couldn't be! But it was ... She stood quite still, the breath stopping in her throat. The cabin should be empty. A shiver of fear chilled her spine.

Someone must have been in the cabin, and recently. Perhaps was still here. Who? If only Larry were with her now. She had been so confident, so adamant that she would be all right. Now she knew she would give much to see the helicopter and the weathered face of its pilot.

Slowly she took the remaining steps to the teahouse. At the door she hesitated, the key in her hand. Should she open it? Should she knock? Neither, she decided, and walked to the lighted window.

There was snow on the pane, but she brushed off just enough with her mittens so that she could peer inside. Her breath stopped again as she saw the man.

He was sitting in an armchair. He had his back to the window, so she could not see his face. He was reading, she thought, and he seemed to be smoking a pipe. From the way his body was angled he had the look of a tall person. She touched the glass again, in an attempt to clear away more snow. And saw him swivel in the chair as he looked towards the window.

Obviously he had been alerted by a sound she had made. Quickly she moved, wedging her body sideways between two shutters. She doubted that he had seen her.

'Now what?' she asked aloud, and saw the breath rising in steam from her lips.

The last thing she wanted to do was go into the cabin. Her sole reason for buying the teahouse had been to get away from people. From men in particular. From viciousness and brutality and deceit. From vulnerability. She never wanted to be vulnerable again.

What am I going to do? she wondered.

In the valley, at the shore of Turquoise Lake, was the hotel. But as she looked at the mountains, at the darkening sky, she knew that she was not going to be able to make her way down the trail before nightfall. Neither could she stay outside in the snow. In her earlier excitement she had not felt the cold but she was aware of it now. It was creeping through her boots, and the exposed parts of her face were rapidly turning to ice. If she remained too long out of doors she would die of exposure.

So she had no option. She would have to go into the cabin. But at least she would be armed.

Face grim now, she went back to her belongings. In the bag of tools was a screwdriver which she shoved into her pocket before returning to the cabin. Let the man turn aggressive and she would have no compunction about jabbing him with the screwdriver. One traumatic experience had been enough for her. From now on she would be prepared.

The door was open. As she stepped inside she heard
a muffled exclamation. And then the man was
uncoiling himself from the armchair. A very tall man,
Cathy saw. Tall and powerfully built. Physically she
would stand no chance against him. Her stomach
muscles tightened as she took the screwdriver from
her pocket.

'Thought I heard something a few minutes ago,' he
said, and Cathy thought he didn't look particularly
surprised to see her. 'Why didn't you come right in?'

She stood as tall as she could, her chin lifted, her
expression assertive. 'I had my reasons.'

An eyebrow lifted momentarily, then he was coming
towards her. 'Well, you're here now, and you look
frozen.'

She took a step back. She held the screwdriver in
front of her, where he could see it. 'Stay where you
are.'

After a moment he said, 'I was just going to invite
you to warm yourself at the fire.' And then, 'So you're
Miss Lennox. You're just a slip of a girl.'

He was expecting an older woman, was he? Who
was he anyway?

Grimly she said, 'Don't let my youth deceive you. I
can take care of myself.'

His eyes were on the screwdriver. 'And harm
yourself into the bargain. Do you think you could put
that implement down? I'm not about to attack you.'

She had not anticipated that Lance, well-dressed,
charming, boyish Lance, would attack her either.
Well, the lesson had been well learned. She would
never put her trust in a man again.

She kept the screwdriver in her hand. 'Who are
you? What are you doing here?'

'I'm Nicholas Perry. I'm from the hotel down at the lake.'

She should have guessed, she supposed. If she hadn't been so frightened she would have guessed. There was something very rugged about the man. He had the fit tanned look of a person who spent much of his day out of doors.

What was it Larry had said? A good man . . . Didn't mean a thing. Men tended to stick together, that was something she had learned at the trial.

'What are you doing here?' she demanded aggressively.

For a moment Nicholas Perry did not answer. Then he said, 'I guess you could say I came up here to welcome you.'

There was a time when Cathy would have smiled and said, 'Thank you, that was kind of you.' But that was in the days before Lance. Before . . . Don't think of it! It's too painful.

Aloud she said, 'It wasn't necessary.' Her tone was as frigid as her expression. She was aware that she sounded ungrateful but that didn't matter. All that mattered was that this man should understand that she was a woman to be reckoned with.

Something flickered in his eyes. In the lamp-light they were dark, but in the day they would be blue, Cathy guessed. And what was she doing even thinking about the colour of his eyes? After today she would not see him again. She intended to make her views quite clear on the subject of uninvited guests.

'I'd say it was extremely necessary.' His gaze rested on her face before travelling down over her figure. 'How long do you think you'd have survived without a fire? Without heat? Without proper arrangements?'

'I'd have seen to all that.'

'Really?' He looked unimpressed. 'You bulldozed Larry into bringing you here against his better judgment. The idea of dropping you in the snow worried him sick.'

'Who told you that?' she asked, though she knew the answer.

'He did, of course. He told you to wait a few weeks. Till spring.'

Yes, men do stick together, she thought. 'It was really none of his concern. Or yours,' she said through tight lips.

'No?' His expression was contemptuous. 'Let something happen to you and the investigations would begin. And then where would Larry be? The irresponsible pilot who should have known better than to abandon an ignorant girl on a snowy mountainside.'

He's not concerned about me at all, she thought, his sole concern is with Larry. She lifted her chin. 'I'm not ignorant.'

'What do you know about survival techniques, Miss Lennox? About being outside in sub-zero temperatures? About bears? There's no telephone up here. What contingency plans have you made for illness, for emergencies?'

Not a single positive answer could she give him to any of those questions. The trouble was that he knew it. What he did not know was her obsession with wanting to get away from Calgary. From the curious looks, from the critical tongues. Lance had been found guilty, yet there were people who thought that Cathy must have encouraged him—which made her the guilty one in their eyes.

'I don't pretend to know everything,' she said

slowly. 'But I'll learn. I can take care of myself.'

Unexpectedly his lips tilted at the corners and she saw amusement warm his eyes. 'With a screwdiver?'

'Unwelcome guests will understand that I'm not defenceless.'

'The odd hikers who make it all the way to the teahouse will be interested only in food,' Nicholas Perry said. 'As for the weirdos—and you'll find those anywhere—I don't know that they would be frightened off by a screwdriver.'

She looked at him levelly. 'I think you're trying to scare me, Mr Perry.'

'If that's what it takes to make you face reality.'

'I faced that some time ago,' she answered him bitterly.

Something in her tone must have got through to him, because he hesitated a moment before saying, 'What about loneliness?'

'I'm not afraid of loneliness.' She looked at him, holding his eyes. 'I enjoy my own company, Mr Perry.'

'My name is Nicholas.'

She didn't rise to that. 'How did you get in?' she asked instead.

'I've always had a spare key. The Mortons never spent the winters up here. You won't either. Someone had to check on things. Though in recent years . . .'

It didn't occur to her to question why he didn't finish the sentence. She was thinking of the cabin. It was true, you couldn't just leave a house in a severe Canadian winter without taking certain precautions, but obviously the Mortons or their agents had done whatever was necessary. She had taken that part of things for granted. Now she was beginning to wonder what she'd neglected, what she needed to know.

There was no reason why Nicholas Perry should know the questions going through her mind. Quite firmly, she said 'I see. Well, you can give me the key now.'

'It's as well for someone to have it.'

And give a man access to her home, her haven? Thank you, but no!

'I don't think so.'

'That's silly,' he said impatiently. 'It's important that someone should be able to get in. You never know when you might need help.'

'I really can take care of myself. I wish you'd believe that.'

He was an attractive man, she admitted to herself. Tall and fair, like a Viking of old, with a shock of untidy fair hair and a strong-boned face, and a beard the same colour as his hair. For a moment she caught herself wondering what his smile would be like. Only to push the thought aside. She wasn't interested in his smile. She wasn't interested in *anything* about him. She only wanted her key and then he could leave.

He was not smiling now. In fact he looked exasperated. 'I can see that you would have worn Larry down with your persistence. You're a stubborn woman, Miss Lennox. There are times when you might not be able to be here, don't you understand that?'

'I wouldn't leave without making adequate arrangements.'

'You shouldn't be here at all.' He looked at her oddly. 'Why don't you just resell the teahouse?'

'No.'

'I'd be happy to buy it from you.'

'Thank you, but no.'

'I'd make it worth your while.'

'You don't seem to understand, Mr Perry. The teahouse isn't for sale.'

Exasperation was etched in every line of the hard-boned face. Finally he said, 'Then go back to Calgary for a while, or stay in the hotel till the snow melts. There'll be no business for you until then.'

'I'm staying here,' she said in the tone of one whose mind was made up. 'Just give me the key, Mr Perry, I'm sure you want to get going.'

She saw his eyes go to the window. 'It's too late for that.'

Cathy went rigid. 'I don't understand.'

'You arrived much later than I expected. It's too late now to walk down the mountain.'

'You can't stay here!' she burst out.

'I have no option. Look outside—there's no way I'd risk that trail in the dark.'

Panic was welling inside her. After Lance had tried to rape her she'd resolved never to put herself in a vulnerable situation again. But she was in one now, and it was a situation not of her making.

'There *must* be a way you can get down.'

'There's no road, only the trail. Even your supplies will have to be brought up by pack-horses.'

She had not wanted to risk the trail herself because it would be dark before she could get half-way along it, so how could she expect him to do it? Yet she couldn't have him here. She was so frightened that she wasn't thinking clearly. But she did not want him to know it.

She looked at him, trying to assess him. He was such a big man, with an unmistakable aura of maleness and strength. She saw it in the powerful body, in the rugged face, in the authoritative manner with which he held himself. He was bigger than Lance, probably stronger than Lance in every way.

'I think you should know,' she said, 'that I've learned some karate.'

He laughed. A very attractive laugh, deep and vital. 'I'm not surprised. You're the most aggressive girl I ever met. Still, I'm glad to hear it. Now I won't let myself worry when I think of you all alone up here.'

She cursed the warmth that flooded her cheeks. 'What I'm trying to say . . .'

'I know what you're trying to say,' he cut in quietly. 'You're in no danger from me, Miss Lennox. I don't know why you're so prickly, but I can tell you that I don't make a habit of forcing myself on women.'

'You get your fun just by asking, I suppose.' She didn't know what made her say it.

'Every time,' he answered her lightly.

And if a woman didn't do what he asked, what then?

There was nothing smooth or slick or movie-star handsome about Nicholas Perry, yet in his rugged way he was extremely good-looking, so she could see women falling for him. Cathy suspected that there was a time when she herself might have found him appealing. And that worried her.

But she was letting her mind drift away from the issues at hand. Though the thought of having him spend the night under the same roof with her was intolerable, it seemed she had no option but to accept it. He couldn't walk down the mountain, nor could he sleep outside, for he would die. Where would he sleep? Well, she would deal with that question when it arose. At least she was prepared. With Lance she had been so naïve, so innocent. So foolishly trusting.

I'll never trust a man again. It was a thought that had come to her again and again in the last four months.

'Where are your things?' Nicholas Perry asked. 'You must have brought some supplies?'

She'd actually forgotten her supplies! That was how preoccupied she'd been with this most disturbing of men.

'They're still where Larry dropped them. I was going to open the house before bringing them inside.'

He reached for his boots and mittens and parka. 'I'll help you.'

She didn't want his help. But it would seem childish to refuse, and it was important that he did not see her as childish. Foolish also to refuse the offer, for a glance towards the window showed her that in the time they'd spent talking it had grown even darker than she had realised.

'Thank you, Mr Perry.'

'Nicholas,' he said as they went through the door.

He seemed to know without being shown where the stuff would have been dropped. In silence they carried everything back to the cabin. It was completely dark by the time the last box had been taken inside.

They took off their heavy outdoor wear and went to the fire to warm their feet and hands. Thank God for the fire, without it the house would have been dark and cold and unwelcoming, Cathy thought, but did not say it.

'Supper,' Nicholas said.

'Yes . . .' Supper? She hadn't thought of this first meal. 'I've plenty of food. I'll get it unpacked.'

'All of it dehydrated?' he asked.

'Some of it. Lots of cans.'

'Just as well I brought a hot meal up with me. There's enough for two people. Do you eat chilli?'

She was cold and tired, and the thought of something warm was sheer bliss. 'Love it,' she said, forgetting to keep up her dignity with him.

'Do we have to have the screwdriver on the table?'

He was smiling, and she saw that it was a smile that made the ruggedness vanish from his face. It warmed his eyes and deepened unexpected laughter lines around his mouth. She had wondered what his smile would be like, now she knew. Even though, she told herself, she didn't want to know.

Damn you, Lance. You've made me hate all men. I'd forgotten that some men aren't hateful. The trouble is, after what you did to me I'll never let myself get to know the nice ones.

She allowed herself a half-smile in return. 'I'll just keep it in my pocket. And . . . thank you, Mr Perry.'

'For what?'

'The fire is marvellous, and you helped me bring in the supplies.'

She's lovely when she smiles, Nicholas thought. She's not nearly as tough and hardbitten as she wants me to think. But what in the world is she doing up here?

'One condition,' he said.

The stiffening was automatic. Did men always have to have their quid pro quo? Well, she wasn't *that* hungry.

'Nick or Nicholas. Not Mr Perry. Nobody calls me Mr Perry.'

She tried the name. 'Nicholas.'

'Is there anything besides Miss Lennox?'

'Catherine.' She swallowed. 'People call me Cathy.'

And that had been difficult for her. She's been hurt, Nicholas realised, and something softened inside him. Who had hurt her, and how? Would she tell him if he asked? No, she would not. She would clam up, and her face would assume that icy mask. She obviously didn't know that it made her look very vulnerable, very young. How old was she anyway? Twenty-two? Twenty-three? At least ten years younger than he was.

'Pretty name,' she smiled. 'Well, now that we have that out of the way, let's see about the chilli.'

As she watched him walk across the room she saw that he limped. She hadn't noticed that before. He'd done a lot of walking if he'd hiked all the way up from the hotel in the snow. And then they'd been in and out of the cold with her things. Perhaps the limp was more pronounced when he was cold and tired.

Careful, she warned herself. Lance had got to her with the little-boy helplessness that had turned out to be an act. She was not going to let Nicholas play on her sympathy. That way lay danger. There was danger enough already in this situation. A man and a woman, alone on a snow-covered mountain, with not a soul in screaming distance.

They ate in the kitchen. It was a big room, a little more dismal than Cathy had expected, but she wasn't worried about that. Her lovely wallpaper would soon brighten it, and ceramics and pot plants would make it cosy.

Nicholas had carried the chilli up the mountain in a thermos, so it was still hot. 'It's good,' Cathy said with the half smile which was as much as she would allow herself.

'It is,' he agreed. 'What were you planning to eat tonight, Cathy?'

She had been much too excited to think about food. 'I would have made a plan.'

'You're good at that, I take it.'

'I think so.'

'I'm glad to hear it. You'll have many plans to make.'

She had been enjoying the meal. Now she was immediately on the defensive once more. 'Trying to frighten me again?'

He grinned, eyes alive and sparkling in the rugged face. 'Now why would I do that?'

'Because it bothers you that I'm here.'

He would deny it, she thought. But he didn't. He looked at her, and it was hard for her to remain unruffled beneath his gaze. It was an intense gaze, taking in much more than surface details. He sees right into me, Cathy thought, with another welling of panic.

'Once you leave here tomorrow you can forget my existence,' she told him, as coolly as she could.

'That might not be easy.'

'Because you feel burdened with responsibility for my well-being,' she said flippantly.

His eyes were enigmatic. 'That's one of the reasons.'

It was becoming more and more difficult to present a façade of calmness. There was an atmosphere in this kitchen. An intimacy . . . And she *hated* it. Nicholas had found some candles and lit them. They gave light to the dismal room. They also created a glow which seemed to draw the two people at the table into a shared island of warmth.

Cathy had to do something to shatter the atmosphere. 'I've had enough to eat,' she said abruptly.

She was standing up when Nicholas caught her wrist. The touch of his hand sent shock ripples through her system. Her heart seemed to thud right into her throat. 'Don't!' The panicked command rang out involuntarily.

'Sit down, Cathy.'

'Let go of my hand! I can't bear to have you touch my hand.' She tried to speak forcefully, and was unaware of the tension in her voice, and the sudden pallor in her cheeks.

He withdrew his hand immediately. 'I wasn't making advances.'

She took a deep breath, hoping to steady herself. Nicholas couldn't know that it was the first time a man had touched her since . . . Don't think about it! Oh, don't think about it. But it was so hard not to.

'Just keep your hands to yourself.' A hint of hysteria remained in her voice.

After a moment he said, 'All right.'

He was puzzled, she saw. And a little hurt. He'd been more than kind really. The trail from the hotel was an upward climb that must take two hours when the ground was dry. Cathy could only guess how long it had taken him to walk through the snow. He'd lit the fire, and brought hot food. And all of it in an effort to make her welcome.

At least—he *said* he wanted to welcome her. How could she be sure? Would a man go to so much trouble for a girl he'd never met, who meant nothing to him?

I've become so distrustful, she thought despairingly. This was what Lance and his assault had done to her.

Perhaps Nicholas really was what he appeared to be on the surface. Rugged and tough, and yet unexpectedly kind. And then again—perhaps he was not. Either way she would never know. She didn't even want to know.

She forced herself to pick up her fork and go on eating. Nicholas ate too. For a while there was silence at the table. A strained silence, for Cathy was uncomfortable, and she suspected there were things Nicholas wanted to say.

Presently he spoke. 'Why did you come here so early?'

Because I couldn't bear to spend another day in the city.

'There are things I want to do before the season starts,' she said.

'Such as?'

'I plan to redecorate.'

'Redecorate?'

'New wallpaper. Pictures. Things like that,' she said lightly. 'And just generally get the feel of the place.'

'I see.' Why was he looking at her so oddly? 'You're going to find it darned lonely.'

'I told you I enjoy my own company.'

'The ability to enjoy being alone is one thing. This . . .' He gestured. 'Living up here like a hermit . . . It's too extreme.'

'Let that be my business.'

'I'm sorry,' he said.

She hadn't expected an apology. Would Lance have apologised? She no longer knew how Lance would have acted in any given situation.

I'm comparing Nicholas with Lance, she thought. And then—will I always make comparisons?

'Why did you buy the teahouse?'

The question, coming after the apology, caught her off guard. She looked at him, and saw that he was really interested. 'I saw it advertised.'

His eyes widened in surprise. 'And you decided to buy it—just like that?'

'I'd been here once. Many years ago.'

The surprise deepened. It was as if Nicholas found it hard to believe what he was hearing. 'Only once?'

'It was enough. I never forgot it. The long trail. The aching muscles and the fatigue. And then coming upon the teahouse, suddenly, here in the trees.'

Nicholas, who for the first time was seeing a hint of the girl beneath the tight tense mask, said, 'Go on.'

'It was the ideal place to stop, of course. We sat out on the patio and had hot soup and home-made bread. It was delicious, but anything would have tasted good after that climb.' She stopped a moment, her eyes suddenly soft with memory. 'There was the view, the glaciers, the lake far below. There was such a spirit of camaraderie. There were other people, strangers, but we all talked and laughed together. We'd all done the climb—that was the common bond.'

This was not the defensive girl who had tried to frighten him with her screwdriver. If only she'd stay this way. 'Sounds as if you enjoyed it,' Nicholas said softly.

'Oh, it was wonderful. I was so happy then.'

'And aren't you happy now?'

It had been the wrong thing to say. The softness left her face and a kind of screen seemed to cover her eyes once more.

She shrugged. 'Happiness is an illusion.'

'That's very cynical.'

'Maybe. It's true too.'

'It doesn't have to be true,' said Nicholas, the man toughened by what life had done to him. For some reason it was suddenly important to reassure the fragile girl opposite him.

'Maybe,' she said again. And then she pushed aside her plate. 'That was good, thank you. Now, if you'll excuse me—I'm going to see the rest of the house.'

CHAPTER TWO

NICHOLAS followed her out of the kitchen.

'You don't have to come with me,' she said.

'I'd like to.'

And what was she to say to that? Could she tell him that she felt a little ill, alone with a man in the dimly lit recesses of a house she did not know at all?

There had been a time in the kitchen when, lulled by memory, she had felt quite relaxed. Certainly more relaxed than she had been with any man since Lance. Now, in the cold bleak passage, strain was mounting inside her again. She was uncomfortably aware of the long hard body behind her. So aware that the little hairs on the back of her neck were standing upright, and she could feel tension charging the air around them. An electric charging. It made her restless and on edge, and she wondered if he felt it too.

He was so big that the little cabin seemed smaller than she'd imagined it. But any house, any room, would seem small when this man was in it. Not that he did anything out of the way to make his presence felt. But it was felt all the same. There was something powerful, something overwhelmingly virile and male and stong about him, so that he seemed to dominate his surroundings.

He would be able to overpower a girl just as easily as a cat could halt a mouse with one movement of its claws. Lance had been much smaller, much slighter, but even then his physical strength had been greater than hers. She could remember her shock, the way she'd sobbed as she'd struggled against him. And suddenly the taste of nausea was bitter on her tongue.

Well, this was one lady Nicholas would not hurt—assuming it was what he had in mind. She had been speaking the truth when she'd mentioned her ability to defend herself. There were things she had learned in the self-defence course she had taken after the attack. Kicks and holds that were supposed to reduce the strongest man to snivelling weakness. Let Nicholas lay a threatening finger on her, and she would have not the slightest hesitation in putting her lessons to practical use.

She put her hand in the pocket of her jeans, curled her fingers around the screwdriver. She hoped she would not have to use it, but the feel of the cold metal was distinctly reassuring.

'Living-room is to your right,' she heard Nicholas say.

She walked in. Only to stop in dismay as she looked around her. Peeling wallpaper covered the walls. The chesterfield—for the Mortons had included their furniture with the purchase—was ancient and dilapidated. In one corner was a pile of old magazines and newspapers, and the floor looked a mess. It was an awful room.

'It will look better in the morning,' Nicholas said sympathetically.

'I guess so.'

But she knew they were both lying. If anything, the bright light of day would emphasise the bedraggled cheerlessness of the place.

The other rooms were no better. The room that Cathy had intended using as a studio for her art-work looked as if it had been neglected for years. It was so depressing that it would actually be an effort to put paintbrush to paper, she thought grimly.

By the time they came to the bedroom she no longer expected anything but the worst. Which was just as well. How anybody could have ever slept in the room was beyond comprehension. Cathy looked around her with disgust. The carpet was a square of fraying strands, and the room had an unpleasant odour. As for the double bed, it leaned to one side and the mattress was sunken.

'No way I'll sleep in that thing,' she said feelingly.

'I don't blame you.' There was compassion in Nicholas's voice. 'But you can't sleep on the floor, Cathy.'

'I brought a sleeping-bag. I'll use that.'

He saw the way her shoulders drooped. Her hair had swung forward, and the slender throat was exposed and vulnerable. She had had a long day—and now this. 'It will look better in the morning,' he said again.

She turned on him. 'Why do you say that?' she demanded. 'You know it won't.'

After a moment he admitted, 'Maybe not.'

'It's a mess. A sheer and utter mess.'

Nicholas looked at her. The gamine face was tired and dejected. She had walked into his life less than an hour ago, a small slim girl, feisty and defiant and brandishing a screwdriver which she seemed quite ready to use. And now, suddenly, the fight appeared to have gone out of her.

'You must have known,' he said curiously.

'No.'

'You really did buy sight unseen then.'

She felt so tired, so terribly tired. 'I told you, I saw it once.'

'Years ago, on a hike. Did you get any further than the table where you ate?'

'No, of course not.'

'Then why?'

'The time was right.' Cathy's voice was low and a little ragged. 'Things were . . . Well anyway, I saw the ad, and it seemed as if it was meant for me to see.'

'All you had was a memory.'

Did he have any idea how precious a memory could be, this vital, virile man who looked as if the good things in life came to him without any effort on his part?

'It was so lovely. The cedar walls. The spirit of the other guests. That incredible view.'

'That's like choosing a gift out of a box because the wrapping is beautiful. And then discovering it's not what you want at all.'

'But I *do* want it.'

'I meant what I said when I offered to buy it from you, Cathy. I'd see that you had a profit as well.'

It must have been sheer fatigue and disappointment that had allowed Cathy to open up to Nicholas. After all her dreams of a wonderful new life the teahouse was a terrible let-down. In the bleak loneliness of the neglected cabin, Nicholas was a flesh-and-blood person, someone to talk to. But his last words brought her back to reality.

'I have no intention of selling.' The challenge was back in her tone. 'Not to you, not to anybody.'

'Sounds familiar,' Nicholas said ruefully.

'What do you mean?'

'Nothing. Go on.'

'This is where I want to be.' Her chin lifted as she looked at him through the gloom. 'Okay, so the place is a mess. I'll clean it.'

'There's a lot to clean.'

'I'll do it all the same.'

She walked to the window. Against the dark sky the snow-covered mountains were indistinct shapes. She turned and looked once more at Nicholas. 'The view is still there. And the cabin itself. It would take a lot more than a little dirt to scare me off.'

He was quiet a few seconds. She stood tensely, not four feet from him, much too aware of him in the silence. It was too dark for her to see his eyes, but already she thought she could guess the expression in them. Strange that, and annoying too, for interest in a man had no part in her plans. But perhaps it was natural in the circumstances that there should be certain features she had committed to memory. Anyway, after today she would not be bothered with his company again.

He laughed suddenly. The sound was low and vital, and disturbingly sexy. Cathy shivered, and despised herself for it.

'You're a feisty lady,' Nicholas said.

'Don't let it bother you.' The calmness of her tone belied the agitation in her system.

'I like it,' he said.

She was beginning to feel claustrophobic. There would never be room for two people in any bedroom of hers, Cathy knew. Once perhaps the knowledge would have made her very sad. Today she accepted that it was the way it had to be for her.

She shrugged, maintaining her façade. 'Let's get

back to the kitchen. I'm going to check on the cleaning equipment.'

'You're not starting to clean tonight, surely?'

'Tomorrow, early—after you've gone.' Her voice was pointed.

'I can take a hint,' he said cheerfully. 'I happen to be zapped. You're not really going to sleep in here, Cathy?'

She suppressed a ripple of distaste. 'Yes, of course.'

'It's cold. I could make a fire, but it would take ages to warm the room.'

'That's okay.'

'Sleep in the kitchen with me.'

'No!'

'Come on, Cathy. It'll be warmer there. More fun.'

Tension was a hard coiled knot in her stomach. She'd rather sit up all night than sleep in the same room with him.

'Fun is not what I'm after,' she told him flatly. 'I'll fetch my sleeping-bag and then I'll say goodnight.'

They went back to the kitchen and she gathered up her personal belongings. At the door she stopped. 'You'll probably leave before I'm awake so I'll say goodbye now.'

A lifted eyebrow was his only answer. Cathy hesitated for an infuriated moment. There were things she would dearly like to say to this man. But there were times when silence was not only more dignified but also safer than speech. And safety from men would always be uppermost in her mind from now on. So she just compressed her lips and walked firmly from the room.

At the doorway to the bedroom she shuddered as the unpleasant odour attacked her nostrils once more.

Heavens, but it was awful. The dirt, the general neglect. The thought of sleeping here filled her with revulsion. Tomorrow, when Nicholas was gone, she would spread her sleeping-bag on the kitchen floor. It was dismal there too, but nowhere near as bad as this bedroom.

A wave of depression swept her, making her limbs so heavy that it was almost too much of an effort to move. It was hard to remember her excitement when she'd spotted the ad for the teahouse.

'Don't go rushing off into the boondocks,' her friend Melissa had said.

'It's not the boondocks, Mel. It's on a mountain above a gorgeous lake. Hikers go there all the time.'

'You'll be lonely,' Melissa's comment was echoed in the sentiment Nicholas had expressed today.

'That's just fine. I want to be alone. I need some time to come to terms with what happened.'

'And then you'll sell the place and come back home?'

'I don't know.' Cathy had been honest. 'At this moment I can't think that far ahead.'

Melissa was a good friend. One of the few people who had stuck to her throughout the dark days of the trial and the time that followed it. Now she looked doubtful. 'You won't be able to attend your therapy group.'

'I'll make my own therapy, Mel. In the teahouse. Cooking and baking for the hikers. Painting. The scenery is so beautiful, I'll never run out of ideas. And I have the children's book to illustrate.'

'You're really set on this project?' Melissa still looked doubtful.

'Absolutely. I feel as if I was meant to see the ad. I

have the money Mom and Dad left me. Of course, that just covers the purchase price, but it won't cost me much to live. Hopefully the teahouse will pay for itself, and there's my art-work. Will you visit me, Mel?'

'If I can get these lazy limbs to do a mammoth climb.'

'It's not that bad.' Cathy had given her a quick hug. 'I'm so excited. Be happy for me.'

Now, as she stood in the gloomy bedroom, Cathy wondered whether anything ever turned out the way one imagined it would be. What high hopes she had had. What plans. The Cathy who had overridden Larry's objections in the helicopter had been optimistic and happy for the first time in many months. And here at last was the reality of her dreams—a cabin that was so dark and dirty and neglected that the very thought of sleeping in it made her feel depressed.

So depressed that her mind went longingly to the kitchen where a cheerful fire was burning. Clutching the sleeping-bag she took a step out of the door. She couldn't sleep in this room, she just couldn't. The kitchen was big, there was plenty of room for two people.

And then she thought of Nicholas. Even without seeing him unclothed she could picture how he would look. Well built, well muscled. A hunk, Melissa would call him. Certainly he was a fine specimen of healthy red-blooded manhood. And red-blooded hunks had only one thing on their minds.

She had no need to think further. There really was no decision to make.

Somehow she summoned the strength to sweep the floor. Only the surface dust came away. The room would need a thorough cleaning to make it habitable, but that would have to wait. In a closet were some newspapers; they were dusty with age, but she spread them over the floor, then put the sleeping-bag down over them. Thank goodness for the sleeping-bag!

Tired as she was, she could not bring herself to lie down right away. She went to the window and looked out into the darkness. Spring had already come in some of the milder parts of Canada but the temperature was still below zero up here in the mountains, and the windows were frozen. In a few weeks it would be warmer. She'd be able to open the windows and let some air into the cabin. The snow would melt and the mountains would be covered with wild grass and alpine flowers. The teahouse would be clean and ready for business. That was the thought to hold on to—all those hikers welcoming the sight of the log cabin at the end of a long and tiring hike.

Things had not turned out as she'd dreamed. But they would. She would see to that. Beginning tomorrow.

She looked at the sleeping-bag again, and her mind went to Nicholas. The very thought of a man sleeping in the cabin with her was enough to fill her with fear. There was a lock on the door, but no sign of a key. Her eyes went to an old chair that stood in the corner of the room. A second later she had put it in front of the door. Let Nicholas try any tricks—the sound of a falling chair would frighten him away. Even if it did not—the noise would waken her, and she would be ready to defend herself.

It really was time to lie down. Her head ached and her arms and legs were sore with fatigue. No matter that the room was a pigsty, a place to lay her head was what she needed more than anything else at this moment. Suppressing a shudder, she got into her pyjamas and crawled into the bag. Things could be worse, she tried to tell herself.

She lay in the down-filled bag and stared out of the bare windows into the dark night. It had started to snow, she could see the falling flakes beyond the frozen pane. Her mind went to the man in her kitchen, but her thoughts made her so restless that she tried to think of the teahouse instead. She was over-tired, she was convinced she would never sleep. But fatigue did get the better of her at last. Heavy lids closed over soft cheeks, and Cathy slept.

In the kitchen Nicholas tried to make himself comfortable, which was no easy feat for a man with a six foot two body and only two chairs to stretch out on. Unlike Cathy he had no sleeping-bag. As he covered his chest and shoulders with his sheepskin parka he spared a longing thought for his comfortable bed in the hotel at the foot of the trail. Which was where he would spend the night tomorrow, he fervently hoped. Perhaps by then he might even have been able to make the girl see some sense.

Not that he held out much hope on that score. Yes, she had been shocked when she'd realised the state the teahouse was in. He could still see the way her shoulders had drooped, and the vulnerable slope of the slender neck. She had recovered quickly enough—or pretended to—but there had been something in her voice that she had been unable to conceal. A rawness, a low huskiness that had not been there before. For a moment he'd detected a slight quivering in her lips.

What a strange girl she was. Prickly as a porcupine ready to throw out its quills when it felt itself threatened. Eventually she had put the screwdriver out of sight, but not out of reach, for he had seen the long thin bulge in the pocket of her jeans. There was something in the way she held the weapon that made Nicholas suspect she had never used it on a man. But there was a look in her eyes that let him know she wouldn't hesitate to give it her best effort if she felt the need.

He'd never met a girl like Cathy. So closed, so defensive. So . . . angry was the word that came to mind. And yet there were moments when he glimpsed something frightened and very innocent.

Buying the teahouse had been the act of someone not only innocent but incredibly naïve. What on earth had possessed her to take it virtually sight unseen, merely because she had once spent a lovely half-hour having hot soup on the sunny patio?

Beneath the prickly exterior she was obviously a romantic. But she would soon be disabused and disillusioned. The elements, the sheer inaccessibility of the teahouse would see to that. She thought she wanted to be alone—had she had an unhappy love affair?—but the reality of the loneliness would be more than she would be able to cope with. She would want to sell the place. And when she did, Nicholas would be there to make a deal.

Uncomfortably, he shifted his long body on the makeshift bed and tried to sleep. And then he heard the screams.

Awful screams. Choked-sounding and terrified. For a long moment Nicholas lay rigid, staring uncomprehendingly into the darkness. And then he jumped from the chairs and was running to the bedroom.

The door was closed. He pushed it open, only to curse as a chair clattered to the floor. He pushed it out of the way with his foot, then stared at the girl in the sleeping-bag.

She was thrashing about. Her arms were flailing, her hands struck the air wildly. And all the time the choked screams came from her throat. The only word Nicholas could make out was 'No.'

He knelt quickly at her side. 'Cathy! Cathy, you're dreaming.'

No response.

'Cathy, wake up.'

The screams increased.

He touched her forehead, then tried to gather her in his arms. But the panicked screams intensified as Cathy hit out more strongly. She was obviously in the grip of some terrible nightmare and felt herself trapped.

'Cathy, wake up. You're only . . . Hell!'

Nicholas moved a fraction away from her, his hand going to his face where she had struck him.

'No!' she was screaming. 'Leave me alone! No! No!'

This was worse than anything he had ever seen. He couldn't leave her like this. And yet he didn't know how to wake her. He watched her carefully, awaiting the moment to imprison her hands, then hitting her once, sharply, on the cheek.

She screamed again. A tortured scream. And then she shuddered and collapsed in a frenzy of weeping.

He let go of her hands and gathered her to him. 'It was a nightmare,' he soothed. 'A bad dream. Wake up, Cathy. Wake up.'

The weeping stopped quite suddenly. And then a small voice said uncertainly, 'Nicholas . . .?'

'Yes, it's only me, Nicholas.'

She was still lying against him. 'What are you doing here?'

'You had a bad dream. You were upset.'

She lay quite still for a moment. And then she jerked up. 'Go away!'

Her change of mood puzzled him. 'Let me stay with you a few moments.'

Her face was wet with sweat and tears, he could feel the moisture through his sweater. Her breath was coming in gasps, like that of a small child who had been crying for hours and was trying, finally, to stop. She was a little like a child herself at this moment, he thought compassionately. A far cry from the tough lady who had walked into the teahouse a few hours ago.

She tried to push herself away from him. 'Go. Please, just go.'

'In a moment. When you're over it.'

He wanted to stay. To hold her. To comfort and protect her. It was the strangest feeling, this wanting to protect her. Nicholas had never experienced anything quite like it before.

'In a moment,' he soothed. 'I just want to hold you.'

He felt the shudder that ran through the fragile body. 'I can't bear to be held.' And then, 'It was just a nightmare. Please go, Nicholas. I'm fine, I really am.'

'If you're sure,' he said doubtfully. Reluctantly.

'Quite sure.' Her voice was husky from screaming, but it was firm too.

He stood up. 'If you need anything, just call.'

She answered him from the floor. 'It won't be

necessary.' He was at the door when she said, 'Nicholas, thank you for everything. I hope you have a good walk down the mountain.'

A thank you was something from this strange girl, he thought as he went back to the kitchen. He had the feeling that thanks did not come easily to her.

He lay back on the chairs, turning this way and that to find a comfortable position. Eventually he looped his long legs over the back of one of the chairs, and thought longingly of the bed that would be his the next night.

The last thought in his mind before he fell asleep was how *good* the small fragile body had felt in his arms.

A strange kind of light filtered through the curtainless window when Cathy woke up. For a few moments she lay quite still. Her head ached and her eyes burned, and her eyelashes had a sticky matted feeling. In the half-conscious state before full wakefulness she wasn't sure where she was or what had happened.

Memory returned quickly. She sat up in the sleeping-bag, her hand clasped to her mouth. When she'd gone to bed the chair had been leaning against the door, now it stood to one side. Nicholas had been in her room during the night. He'd pushed away the chair. And he'd held her in his arms. She remembered him holding her. And the memory made her feel ill.

What could he have thought of her? Not that it mattered. By now he would be half-way down the mountain, if not back at the hotel. She would not see him again for a few weeks, not until she went to the hotel to arrange for supplies to be sent up to the teahouse. Perhaps she would not have to see him even then.

What upset her far more than Nicholas's opinion of her, was that once more her privacy had been violated. She'd put the chair against the door for a purpose. And he had pushed it aside with no trouble at all. She was not concerned with his reasons for doing so. The fact was that once more she had been at a man's mercy.

She shivered as she began to get out of the sleeping-bag. God, but it was cold! The temptation was to get right back into it, to cuddle up and pull the hood over her head. And stay cocooned and warm until summer, she thought wryly. Safe and warm and isolated.

Only that was not the way it could be. Her eyes went to the grimy floor and the peeling walls and the tattered lampshade covering the only light in the room. She'd come to the teahouse with visions of making it attractive before the beginning of the season. Now she knew that the first priority was just to get it clean.

Teeth chattering, she pulled on some clothes and went to the bathroom. Thank goodness she would not have to see Nicholas again. Still, without him she would have had problems. No heat in the cabin, no light, no water flowing through frozen pipes. Had she thanked him adequately for his help? She couldn't be sure.

Surprisingly the water was warm, if not hot, and after a shower she felt somewhat restored. When she had delved in her suitcase for a fresh pair of jeans and a cuddly rose-coloured sweater, and had run a brush through tangled hair, she felt ready to face the day.

She was hungry. What would she eat? A little of last

night's left-over chilli? She pulled a face. No, not that. Today she would have to get herself organised. Decide how she was going to cope with her stock of food until Larry's next drop-off of supplies. Make a list of the things that had to be done to the teahouse, and then decide on her priorities.

She was actually smiling as she left the bedroom. Last night she had felt terribly depressed, for nothing had gone as she'd hoped. This morning everything looked different. Okay, so the teahouse was a mess. But she was strong and healthy and she had lots of time. A temporary set-back was not going to affect the life she had planned for herself.

She came into the kitchen. And stopped. Nicholas was there, a tall figure, superbly built, standing looking out of the window.

Cathy's happy mood vanished in a second. 'Nicholas?'

He turned, and she saw that he was holding a mug with steam rising from the top of it. 'Good morning.'

'Good morning,' she managed to say in return. And then, 'What are you doing here? I thought you'd be gone by now.'

'Sorry to disappoint you.' His grin was wicked. Attractive too. 'Fancy some coffee?'

'Yes ... Thank you.' The thanks were an afterthought, and his deepening grin told her that he knew it.

A kettle was boiling on the stove, and she watched as he spooned some instant coffee into a mug, then poured the boiling water over it.

'How did you know where to find the coffee?' she asked as he handed her the mug.

'Went through your boxes.'

'Not shy, are you?' was her wry comment.

'When it comes to survival—no.'

She clasped her hands around the warm mug. 'Men always look out for themselves.'

He gave her a look that was penetrating yet amused. 'You're a cynical girl.'

'I have reason to be,' she shot back at him.

'Why?'

She stared at him, taken aback by his directness. After a moment she said, 'It's really none of your business.'

'Hm.' He took a sip of his coffee. And then he asked, 'How was your night?'

Her chest felt tight. She looked away from him as she queried carefully, 'Why do you ask?'

'Because I'm concerned.'

'I don't need your concern,' she said brittly. 'Talking of which, I put the chair against my door for a reason. You had no right to come bulldozing your way in.'

'I think you know why I came in,' he said, quite gently.

She had expected him to be hostile in return. His gentleness caught her off guard. A little uncertainly, she said, 'I guess I had a dream.'

'A very bad dream, Cathy. A nightmare.'

'We all have nightmares,' she countered, with a touch of her earlier aggression.

'This one must have been a real whopper. You were screaming, that was what brought me running. When I got to you, you seemed very distressed.'

'It was just a nightmare,' she said again. 'Anyway, I don't want to talk about it.'

'Do you remember it?'

'Don't you understand? I don't want to talk about it.'

'What was it about?'

Would he never stop? 'I don't have the slightest idea.'

Liar. She knew exactly what the nightmare had been about. She could have described it to him in minutest detail. The man creeping up on her. Capturing her from behind. Her struggles. And the realisation, the utterly helpless and terrible realisation, that he was too strong for her.

'Tell me,' Nicholas said.

This had been her first nightmare in at least two weeks. Ever since she'd known she was coming to the Rockies there had been the teahouse to think about, to look forward to. A new life. She had been so happy, so excited, that the nightmare had stayed away.

She knew what had brought it back. Nicholas. The strange man in her house. Too big, too strong, far too damned sure of himself. Even with the chair against the door—and how little use that had been when she'd needed it!—she had felt threatened.

'There's really nothing to tell.' She was beginning to feel agitated. And the lovely happiness of half an hour ago was dissipating just as if it had never existed.

She was making for the door, knowing only that she had to get away from him, when it happened. Suddenly. Unexpectedly.

He reached for her, his hand capturing her chin— such a huge hand, the palm of it slightly roughened. She could feel every one of his fingers against the soft skin of her face.

Nausea welled inside her. Panic made her heart double its regular beat, so that the pulse in her throat beat against that big man's palm like a bird fluttering desperate wings against the bars of a cage.

'Tell me,' Nicholas said.

She tried to talk but her throat was closed, her mouth was dry. At last, with an effort that was almost superhuman in its intensity, she managed to summon the words, 'Get the hell out of here!'

'Cathy . . .'

Strength was returning to her limbs. She lifted her hand and wrenched at his with all the power that was in her. And was surprised to find how easily his hand came away. He really wasn't holding her tightly at all. Not like Lance, who had tried to overpower her with his greater physical strength. Not like the man in the nightmare.

Free of him, she took a few steps away. She faced him, a little crouched. Like a small wounded animal, thought Nicholas, and once more he felt something soften inside him.

'I don't want to talk about it.' The words came out in something like a sob.

'All right,' Nicholas said at length.

'Just go.'

'I can't.'

'You don't understand. I want you out of my house.'

'I'm going nowhere,' Nicholas said. 'At least not today.'

CHAPTER THREE

CATHY stared at him appalled. 'What did you say?'

Nicholas's eyes were narrowed. He was watching her intently now. 'That I will be going nowhere today.'

She felt trapped. Terror gripped her once more, turning her skin to ice. 'I don't understand.'

'Have you looked out of the window this morning?'

'No.'

'Then I suggest you do.'

When she didn't move, he came towards her, holding out a hand. 'Come.'

'Don't touch me!'

She had drawn back. She was against the wall now, she'd moved as far away from him as was possible. The colour that had been in her cheeks earlier had drained from them, leaving her face pale and wan, making her look even younger and more vulnerable than ever.

Nicholas, who had never met anyone like Cathy, dropped his hand. 'I'm just asking you to take a look out of the window.'

She went on standing there, looking at him, her hands a little in front of her, as if she was warding off some invisible danger.

His mouth hardened. 'Nothing's going to happen to you. Besides, you have your damn screwdriver.'

In fact Cathy had left the screwdriver in the pockets of her other jeans, in the bedroom. But Nicholas had no way of knowing it. Well, a good bluff was a fine weapon any day, that was one of the things the instructors in the self-defence course had taught her.

'Right. And remember it.' Some of the feistiness of the previous night was in her tone.

'I'll remember. Now come to the window.'

She went then. She walked across the kitchen, head held high, shoulders squared, the look on her face as self-assured as she could make it. If Nicholas knew that she was scared of him, his power over her would be infinite. It was time to dispel any impression of weakness she might have given him.

Beyond the cabin lay a winter-fairyland. There were the mountains she had seen yesterday, tall and towering and majestic. Close by were the pine trees, dark splashes of green against the snow. Snow was everywhere. Thick and white and untouched-looking. It was snowing right now, big flakes falling slowly, silently, to the ground. Alone at the window Cathy would be able to spend a long time enjoying the view. But Nicholas was with her—keeping a respectful distance this time—and that spoiled everything.

'Well?' he asked at last.

She kept her face turned away from him. 'I'm not sure what you're trying to show me.'

'You must see all the snow.'

'Of course.'

'You don't understand, do you? There was a blizzard last night, Cathy.'

She remembered watching the white flakes beyond the window from her sleeping-bag. 'I know it snowed.'

'It was much more than that. It came up during the night. High winds and drifting, you must have been sleeping by then.'

She understood what he was getting at, of course. 'You know your way down the mountain, Nicholas. You live here.'

'It's still snowing,' he said inexorably.

'It shouldn't matter.'

'Either you're incredibly naïve, or else you're unconcerned about anyone's welfare but your own,' he said in a hard tone.

The words stung her. She swung round. 'That's not true.'

'We've had more than a foot of snow since yesterday. And as you see it's still coming down.'

She kept her chin high, hiding her unhappiness, and knowing even without hearing what he had to say that she had to accept the inevitable. 'Yes, I see. I guess you will have to stay.'

'There's a snow-drift three feet high banked up against the front door.'

She met his gaze, and saw how steady his eyes were. Attractive eyes—the thought flashed unwillingly through her mind—wide and very blue, just as she'd guessed yesterday they would be. There was something far-seeing in those eyes, the eyes of a man who had spent years of his life scanning high mountain slopes. There was something open in the eyes too—on the face as a whole, come to think of it. Open and direct, as if Nicholas was a man who scorned deceit and the small sly things in life.

She was about to smile at him. And then stopped. Was she insane that she thought herself able to judge a man by the face he presented to the world? She had been so wrong about another man.

'Does it mean we can't get out of the cabin at all?' she asked at last.

'The back door isn't in the path of the wind and there's no drifting there.'

A space of at least two feet separated them, and yet Cathy was as acutely aware of Nicholas's long strong body as if she were touching it. It was a feeling that made the hair on her neck prickle with nervousness. But there was another sensation too. One that had been missing last night. She pushed it to the back of her mind, refusing to analyse it.

She looked away from the hard-boned face and let her eyes rest on the snowy landscape once more. 'Then we're not altogether trapped.'

'We can get out of the cabin if that's what you mean.'

Cathy let out a small breath of relief. 'Thank goodness for that.'

'Not that there's anywhere you can go.'

'Not down the mountain, but I need to know that I can get out.'

'I wouldn't advise it,' Nicholas said. 'You must know what blowing snow can be like. You're a stranger here, you'd become disorientated in minutes and never find your way back to the cabin.'

'I wouldn't go far,' Cathy replied. 'I just need to know that I can catch a breath of fresh air when I want to. I'd go crazy in here if I couldn't get out.'

'Where is the girl who said loneliness would be no problem? That she enjoyed her own company?' There was an unexpected bubble of laughter in his voice.

She looked at him, then looked quickly away. Oh, but he was unsettling, this big bearded man with the hard face and the attractive laugh. There was a powerful maleness that clung to him as if it was as much a part of him as his skin. She had hoped that in coming to this isolated spot in the Rockies she would forget what had happened. Instead, since yesterday afternoon, it was constantly on her mind. She was no longer as frightened of Nicholas as she had been yesterday, but for the sake of her sanity she knew she would need an occasional break from his company.

'Didn't you mean what you said about loneliness?' Nicholas asked, and she realised that she hadn't answered his question.

'I'm not alone now,' she said pointedly, and heard the hiss of his breath.

'Whatever you might think, I'm not a monster, Cathy.'

'No,' she admitted unwillingly.

And, strangely, she knew it was true. Nicholas was not a monster. Not on the surface anyway. And that was the problem. Lance had seemed harmless enough. He'd been charming, attentive, fun. To Cathy, unsuspecting and so very trusting, the assault had come as a shock. And so with Nicholas she was prepared. There was nothing he could do that would surprise her. This time she was prepared for the worst.

'More coffee?' he asked.

'Please.'

She took the mug he gave her, warming the palms of her hands with its heat. It was good coffee, strong and hot. There was also a piece of crusty bread and cheddar cheese.

'You must have carried more up the mountain than I realised,' she said.

'I didn't think dehydrated food was the most appealing way to start a new life.'

'Yuk.'

The word had come out feelingly. After a moment she smiled at him, and he smiled in response. Their eyes met, held. Cathy was the first to look away. Nicholas would be an easy man to like. Too easy. It was not what she wanted. On the other hand, perhaps she had been unnecessarily churlish. She could maintain a measure of friendliness without surrendering her control.

'I don't think I really thanked you yesterday,' she said, a little awkwardly.

His grin deepened. 'I don't think you did.'

'It was kind of you to go to so much trouble.'

She saw the amusement in his eyes, the way his lips lifted at the corners. His smile chased the strong-boned hardness from his face.

'Very kind,' he mocked.

She was beginning to feel foolish. 'I mean it.'

'I just find it hard to believe that we're really conducting this very polite social conversation.'

How did we get into this? she wondered. And knew she had to go on.

'The food is the least of it. I could have been without light. Without water. I guess I took a lot for granted.'

'Yes,' he said softly. 'You did.'

There was something—a kind of tenderness—in the way he said the words, and she didn't like it. Hardness, rudeness, those she could deal with. Tenderness was something else. She felt shaken. Vulnerable. And she didn't want to feel vulnerable ever again.

With a hint of yesterday's defiance, she lifted her chin. 'I would have managed though.'

'I think that's true.'

'Don't try to humour me, Nicholas.' She was beginning to feel angry. 'Okay, I admit there are things I don't know. Things I should have known. But I would have learned. And I'd have come through on my own.'

'Sure you would have. I told you yesterday that you were a feisty lady.'

She threw him a look. But he was neither mocking nor humouring her. 'Anyway—I just wanted to say thanks.'

'You're welcome. It's no more than I'd have done for any neighbour.'

Any neighbour . . .

She sipped her coffee. For a while they were silent. The first comfortable silence they had shared. There were other things to be said, but for the moment they could wait.

Cathy looked around her. Nicholas had added fresh wood to the fire. It was burning high, the flames throwing coppery lights across walls and floor. But even the cosiness of the fire did not detract from the shabbiness of the room. In the clear light of day it looked even bleaker than when she'd seen it yesterday.

'The whole place is a mess,' she said at last.

'Uh-huh.'

'I'm surprised it wasn't condemned.'

'It would have taken a hardy inspector to climb the trail to investigate.'

'I'll start with the kitchen. If I'm going to cook for other people this area should be clean.'

'Sensible idea.'

She saw the way his hand curled around his mug. It was broad and tanned, the fingers were long. There was strength in that hand. Competence. The same strength and competence that she'd sensed in him ever since their meeting yesterday. Cathy did not have to visit Turquoise Lake Hotel to know that it would be well run and successful. Nicholas Perry was a man who would not tolerate incompetence in himself or in those he employed.

'The other rooms are even worse. They're really awful, Nicholas. How could the Mortons live like this?'

'I don't think the mess worried them.'

'It worries me,' she said grimly.

'There *is* a solution.'

She looked up quickly. 'I wouldn't think of selling.'

His eyes were on her, penetrating, intent. She felt her heart beat suddenly faster, and wasn't sure why. 'You want this place so badly?' he asked.

'Yes.'

'Why?'

Tense now, she wondered whether he knew about Lance. But he didn't know, she realised a moment later. If he did, his manner towards her would have been different from the start.

Coolly she replied, 'That's my business.'

He shrugged. 'As you wish.'

She saw the tightening of his lips. Okay, so he found her strange. Cold, brittle, stand-offish. Unfeminine. Better by far than that he should think her weak. And yet . . . it was oddly disturbing that he should see her in such an unattractive light.

Silence fell once more. Cathy drank her coffee, and ate the rich home-made bread, but with less enjoyment now. The exchange had revealed something to her. She did not want Nicholas to find her unappealing. The logical part of her saw the need for it. But there was a part of her that Lance had not succeeded in destroying, a part that wanted Nicholas to find her attractive even while she recognised the foolishness of such a wish. For there could never be a life for her with a man, not the way she felt about men in general. And so the teahouse, for all its messiness and isolation, was the place where she would find happiness. She would clean it, decorate it. It would be *her* place. Her own special haven. She just wished that she could shake off her feeling of unhappiness.

Beneath her lashes she looked once more at Nicholas. Physically he was an attractive man. And she wondered how it would be to make love with him. It was a wondering that came quite of its own, it was difficult to push away. Before Lance, Cathy had enjoyed her sexuality, limited though her experience had been. That part of her life was over now—it had to be over—yet it seemed that she could still recognise the sexual earthiness in Nicholas.

Uneasily she shifted in her chair. She would be glad when it stopped snowing, when Nicholas could leave here. He was a definite threat to her peace of mind.

She stood up and walked to the sink. With her back to Nicholas, she asked, 'Won't your wife mind your staying up here with me?'

'I'm not married.'

He had given her the answer to her real question, not to the one she had asked. For what she had really wanted to know was whether he was married. And now that she knew—what of it? There was a time when the knowledge might have pleased her. Had she met Nicholas in that time before Lance, she might have regarded him differently. *Would* have regarded him differently, she admitted honestly to herself. But now, whether he was married or not meant nothing to her. Less than nothing.

When she had rinsed the breakfast things, Cathy brought out her cleaning equipment and filled a pail with warm soapy water.

'Wasting no time,' Nicholas commented from somewhere behind her.

'There's lots to do. I'll try not to get in your way.'

He made an amused sound, and she felt herself colour. He seemed to have a way of robbing her of her poise. 'You could read or something,' she said defensively. 'You were reading when I arrived.'

'A thriller I found in a pile of old books.'

'You must be dying to know how it goes on.'

'I've read it before.' He laughed. 'Come on, Cathy, drop the primness, you know I'm going to help you.'

So he thought she was prim. 'You don't have to.'

'Of course not,' he said easily, 'but you know I will all the same. I take it you want to start with the kitchen.'

'Yes . . .'

His matter-of-factness told her it was useless to argue with him. In a surer tone, she said again, 'Yes.'

'Let's begin by moving the furniture out of here.'

'Okay.'

The furniture, like everything else the Mortons had left behind in the cabin, was old and shabby. When they had taken the chairs to the living-room, it was back to the kitchen. Nicholas lifted one end of the table, and after a moment Cathy lifted the other end. She met his eyes across the length of the table, and saw that his lips had lifted slightly at the corners. She thought he would speak but he didn't, and she was silent too. But as they began to walk across the kitchen floor, their steps matching, something shivered inside her. For Heaven's sake, they were just moving a table together. The most routine of chores. It was idiotic that she should feel a sense of togetherness.

But the feeling persisted.

For hours they worked in virtual silence. They could have talked, Cathy supposed, but she did not want to. She had nothing to talk about with Nicholas. And so when he began scrubbing walls on one side of the kitchen, she made a point of being on the other side, as far away from him as was possible. And if he thought she was unfriendly, it didn't matter. The moment of togetherness had unsettled her more than she wanted to admit to herself. She was not ready to repeat it.

It must have been mid-day when Nicholas said, 'Feel like breaking for a while?'

'If it's what you want.' If *you* are tired, her tone implied.

If he was at all disconcerted by her manner he did not show it. 'Sure. I'll cut some more of the bread and the cheese. Why don't you put on the kettle?'

Without argument for once, she did as he suggested. She had a feeling that some of her arguments yesterday and today had sounded childish to him, and that was something she regretted. But Nicholas could not know her dread of appearing vulnerable, he could not guess the lengths she would go to in order not to appear defenceless.

They ate their lunch in the kitchen, spreading it out on the counter. By tacit mutual consent they did not go to the table in the living-room, the bleak cold room would have been too depressing. By contrast the kitchen was cheerful. There was still lots to be done but the walls were clean now and so was the counter. And the fire which Nicholas kept lit was warm and bright and made soft crackling sounds.

Nicholas leaned against the counter, one long leg stretched across the other. Cathy hitched herself on to the Formica top, letting her feet dangle down.

'Am I allowed to say that you look like a teenager?' Nicholas asked.

Yesterday she would probably have bristled at the question. But today she was beginning to feel a little differently towards Nicholas. He could so easily have taken advantage of her during the night. And he had been very helpful today, scrubbing as hard as she did, cheerfully, without a single sarcastic remark or complaint.

'I suppose you can, though actually I'm a mature woman of twenty-three.'

'Impossible,' he teased.

She smiled back at him. 'Yes. Actually, it's a joy to get the weight off my feet.'

'We could have stopped earlier.'

'I didn't realise till now how tired I am.'

'Well, it's good to know you're human. I was beginning to wonder.'

The smile vanished from her eyes. 'Oh, I'm human all right.'

He shot her a quick look. 'Did I say something I shouldn't have?'

'No.' It came out a little too quickly.

'I think I did. Won't you tell me what it is?'

Without warning his hand touched hers. His fingers burned her skin, and she shuddered. Abruptly she pulled her hand away.

'Cathy ...' He looked puzzled. Even a little

distressed, though she was too distraught to notice that.

'I think . . .' I think it's time to get back to work, she had been about to say. But her feet ached, and the calves of her legs were stiff. She wasn't used to work that involved hours of standing, and every nerve and muscle seemed to cry out in protest. Much as she wanted to get away from Nicholas, she had no option but to remain where she was—for a little longer at least.

'What's wrong?' Nicholas asked.

'Nothing.' From somewhere she dredged up a brittle smile. 'Really.'

'All I did was touch your hand.'

'Right. I told you it was nothing.'

'Then why do you act as if you were about to be raped?'

'Don't try it.' At the word the colour had drained from her cheeks. 'I'd fight like crazy if you tried to rape me.'

'With the screwdriver.' His eyes were watchful.

'Not only the screwdriver. With what I've learned about self-defence I'd be safe from you.'

'You're safe anyway, because I don't go in for rape.' The smile had left his face. 'It was only a touch on the hand, Cathy.'

She was trying very hard to get her breathing under control. Not for anything did she want him to see how the conversation was affecting her.

'Perhaps that's all it was to you,' she said.

'That is all it was, period.'

She did not know what to say to that, so she remained silent. His eyes were still on her face, watchful, penetrating. If she was not careful he could see things she did not want him to see. Not Nicholas, not any man. She turned her own eyes towards the window, and saw that it was still snowing.

When he spoke again his voice had changed. It was gentle, as if he realised that she was upset, and wanted to soothe her. 'I'm sorry—I seem to be getting on your nerves.'

'No . . .'

Rather incredibly, it was true. In some strange way which she didn't fully understand, there was a part of her which was glad of his presence here. He brought life and vitality into the bleak loneliness of the cabin. If only she weren't so frightened . . .

He took a few steps away from her, giving her the space she needed. 'I really can't go, you know.'

'Yes, I know.'

'If I could get down the mountain I would.'

'Well, of course. There's nothing to keep you here.'

She expected him to agree. Strangely he didn't. A silence followed her words. An odd, tense kind of silence. She caught an expression in his eyes, but it was gone so quickly that afterwards she wondered if she had imagined it. She felt restless, unnerved.

The silence continued so long that she knew she had to break it. 'This is a bit like a picnic.' She tried to smile, and felt as if her face was cracking.

'I guess it is.' With relief she saw that he was smiling too.

She glaced at the window. 'It's still snowing.'

'It will stop, you know. It always does. And then you'll be rid of me.'

It was said without malice. He knew how she felt, though she did not think he knew why. He was kind, this tall bearded man. At least she *thought* he was kind. Since Lance there was always the afterthought.

Cathy could have taken the rest of the day off. It would have made no difference to the end result, and she knew it. It would be quite some time before the first hikers could be expected to arrive at the teahouse. But it was as if demons were driving her on. Despite her tired muscles, she was too on edge to relax, too restless to curl up in one of the shabby old chairs that the Mortons had left behind. As she slid off the kitchen counter she wondered if she would feel any different if Nicholas were not with her.

With the walls and the counter done, she decided to make a start on the floor. It was covered with lino, thick with many layers of old wax. Cathy surveyed it with distaste, then she got on to her knees and began to strip it.

'Just as well that I thought of bringing wax and strippers with me,' she muttered.

Nicholas took himself off to the living-room, to sandpaper the walls. Alone in the kitchen, Cathy felt immediately more relaxed. No male eyes following her around the room, studying her. No male presence filling her with an uncomfortable awareness.

She tried to visualise the teahouse as it would be when she had cleaned and decorated it. And found herself thinking of Nicholas instead. He was an attractive man, no doubt about it. Strong and self-confident. Good-looking in that rugged, outdoor way. Lean lithe body, but powerful with it. For a few treacherous moments the old Cathy, the Cathy who had had a healthy interest in the male sex before Lance, wondered how that body looked without clothes. As for the beard—she had never been kissed by a man with a beard. Did it tickle?

And then the new Cathy caught herself short in disgust. Idiot! she thought, appalled. What the heck was she doing? Letting herself wonder about Nicholas Perry was really absurd. She was done with men. She was on the threshold of a new life, one that would be rewarding and happy. And it would be a happiness of her own making. She would depend on nobody but herself.

Still—it was not easy to push Nicholas from her mind, and her thoughts gave her little comfort.

As if hard work might rid her of her unwanted thoughts, she invested her chores with more energy than was necessary. At last the floor was stripped. A new floor was what was really needed, for here and there it was showing the signs of wear that were evident everywhere in the cabin, but it would have to wait until she could afford it. In the meanwhile, a thin layer of new wax and much tender loving care would have to do.

By the time Cathy was ready to wax it was mid-afternoon, and a glance out of the window revealed the bleakness of the wintery landscape. She would finish the floor, and then she would put on the kettle she had taken to the living-room. From that room came the sound of scraping. Nicholas would also be ready for coffee. She began to apply the wax, cautiously at first, and then with more confidence. It was the first time she had waxed a floor, for in her apartment in Calgary the floors were either carpeted or ceramic. There was only one corner left to do, and she was feeling really proud of her work when she looked up. Only to let out a gasp.

'Shoot!'

The exclamation brought Nicholas to the door of the kitchen. 'Something wrong?'

'I'm afraid so.'

He took in the scene in a moment. And then he let out a shout of laughter. 'Oh Cathy, what have you done!'

'Boxed myself in,' she said ruefully.

'With a vengeance.'

'It isn't funny.' But her smile belied her words. 'You don't know how hard I worked, I stripped years off this floor before putting on the new wax.'

'It looks great.'

'Stop laughing, Nicholas.'

'Who's laughing?' He put his hands to his mouth, pretending to tug the laughter from his face. 'Do you think I would be so rude? Are you going to stay there till it's dry, Cathy?'

'It's almost dry now, but if I walk on it I'll spoil it. God, I'm dying for a cup of coffee.'

'I think you need a knight to the rescue.' He was laughing again.

She looked at him doubtfully. 'There's nothing you can do.'

'Sure there is. Get on the counter. Right ... Now edge your way to the side.'

She did what he said, only to stop when she reached the edge of the counter. 'It's no use, Nicholas. I can't jump from here.'

'With my help you can.' He held out his arms to her.

'No.' She pulled back.

'Don't be scared. I'll catch you, I promise.'

She was still hesitant. 'You might not.'

'You can take a chance on it, or you can stay there till the wax is quite dry.'

That decided it. She was tired and she wanted her coffee, and she was not going to remain on this hard counter a moment longer than she had to.

'Of course if you miss, and this lovely floor is horribly marked, you'll rewax it for me,' she said.

'It's a deal. Okay, Cathy, let's see you jump.'

Cathy, tomboy of yesteryear, had jumped from many a tree when she was young. She took a breath, and launched herself away from the counter.

A pair of arms reached for her. Caught her. Swung her easily over the precious wax and through the open doorway.

'Good girl!' Nicholas exclaimed.

She looked up at him. 'Thanks.'

He looked down at her. 'For what?'

In that moment she realised that he was still holding her. His hands were on her waist, her body was just inches from his. She was about to pull away when he said softly, in a tone she had not heard him use before, 'Cathy . . .'

Panic welled inside her. But she kept her voice under control. 'You can let me go now.'

He didn't. His hands left her waist only so that his arms could go around her. Now she could feel the hard long length of him against her. And she *hated* it. She felt as if she was being stifled. She would have screamed if the breath hadn't choked in her throat. She had to get away from him quickly.

But for a moment her body was unable to move. And in that moment he brought one of his hands to her chin. Before she could react he had tilted her face towards his, and then he was kissing her.

It was really quite a gentle kiss but she was trembling violently, every nerve rebelling against what was happening. Adrenalin shot through her system, and she pushed Nicholas so hard that he lurched backwards and into the wall behind him.

'You little hell-cat!' he ground out. 'What brought that on?'

'Keep away from me!'

'It was just a kiss.'

She was pale and breathing hard. 'Don't try it again.'

'It was just a kiss between friends.' He was reaching for her again, when he saw that she had raised her knee. Hastily he backed away.

He eyed her from a distance. 'You wouldn't . . .' he said, but warily.

'Oh yes I would,' she countered. She was still trembling but the fact that he was keeping his distance gave her some measure of satisfaction. 'I will not be molested.'

'It was just a kiss,' he protested again.

'That's how it starts. I won't be molested, Nicholas. Not by you. Not by anyone.'

For long moments they eyed each other across the dark passage. Nicholas had recovered his composure. His eyes were narrowed, thoughtful. It was hard to know what he was thinking. Cathy watched him tensely. Her body was taut, as if she was ready to attack or defend.

Finally Nicholas said softly, 'I think you have a problem.'

It was the unexpected gentleness in his tone that was her undoing. It was the one weapon she had not anticipated. She looked at him a moment longer. Then her face crumpled, and she ran to the bedroom.

'Cathy!' she heard him shout.

She didn't answer him as she banged the door shut and leaned against it, as much to keep him out as for support. Now that the threat had passed she felt drained. Empty. Numb. And sad. So terribly sad.

There was no sound behind the door. Obviously he had decided not to come after her. All the fight suddenly going out of her, she threw herself on to her sleeping-bag and wept.

CHAPTER FOUR

SHE wept as she had not wept since she was little. She wept for Lance and the hurt he had done her. She wept for the trauma she had endured as a result. And she wept, most of all, for the person she had become. For months she had kept her emotions tightly in check, had never allowed herself the luxury of tears. It had taken Nicholas, and a kiss, to undermine her defences.

It was only when the paroxysm of weeping had abated that she realised how cold she was. There was no fire in the room and she was dressed lightly. She got up and put the chair in front of the door—a symbolic barrier, nothing more, for it would not keep Nicholas out if he meant to come in. At best the falling chair would give her a few moments in which to marshal her defences. And then she pulled on her parka and crept into her sleeping-bag.

There wa a knock at the door. She chose to ignore it. She did not want to see Nicholas. If she never saw him again she would be content.

'Cathy,' he called. 'Cathy, come out.'

She said nothing.

'Cathy, please. I'm sorry if I upset you.'

Still she remained silent. Perhaps she was being childish but she didn't want to see Nicholas. She wasn't ready for it. If only it would stop snowing and he would just vanish from her life. A futile wish. Even if the snow were to stop falling this minute, it was almost dark. There could be no going down the mountain tonight.

She heard his footsteps as he walked away from her room. Evidently he understood that she wanted to be alone, and had decided to respect her wishes. And that was something, she had to admit to herself. Lance wouldn't have given a damn.

It was hunger and thirst that eventually forced her out of the room. Her throat was raw from all her tears, and she was so hungry that her stomach rumbled and ached. What would Nicholas say when he saw her? Well, she didn't really care what Nicholas thought or said. She would try to maintain a cool dignity—if that was possible after what had happened—and hope like crazy that by tomorrow he would be gone.

He was in the kitchen, reading. He looked up when he saw her, and she braced herself. Now would come the questions.

He put down his pipe and his book and smiled at her. His only question was, 'Like some coffee?'

Her throat was so raw that it hurt to swallow. 'Love some.'

He stood up and went to the stove where a kettle was boiling on low heat. 'I thought you might.'

She was still standing in the doorway when he brought her a mug. Gratefully she took a sip. Then she came into the room and drew up a chair at the fire.

'I see you brought the furniture back into the room.'

'Had to do something to make myself useful.'

She forced a smile. 'You've done quite a bit.'

It wasn't quite what she had meant to say, but somehow the words came out of themselves. Nicholas was kind. Whatever else he might be, she had to admit that he was kind.

'You must be hungry,' he said.

'Starved.'

'How do frankfurters and mashed potatoes sound to you?'

The smile was easier this time. 'Pretty good.'

She watched as he opened the oven and brought out the food.

'I decided to go to your supplies again,' he said. 'I didn't think you'd mind.'

'No, of course not. Aren't you going to have any?'

'I've eaten.'

'Oh. Yes, you would have.'

She began to eat, and realised that she was even hungrier than she'd imagined. She kept her eyes down, glad of the excuse not to look at him.

At last she said, 'What time is it?'

'Seven-thirtyish.'

So she'd been in the sleeping-bag a long time. Nicholas must be curious, he wouldn't be human if he wasn't. But he was keeping his questions to himself, and for that she was grateful.

'The kitchen looks good,' she said eventually, to break the silence.

'It looks great. Amazing what a bit of scrubbing can do for a room.'

'It will look even better when I've wallpapered it.'

'Sure will.'

'It's an off-white wallpaper with a bit of blue in it.'

'Nice.'

'I have some lovely delft plates in storage in Calgary. I'll hang a shelf on that wall by the window. They'll look good there.'

'I have a feeling the whole cabin will look good,' Nicholas said quietly.

Cathy went on eating. Her eyes were still down, and she was trying very hard to keep her hands from shaking. Did Nicholas sense the effort she was making? Yes, she thought, he did. He seemed to be an unusually perceptive man.

'I think it will look good. I plan to . . .' She stopped. She was talking too much because she didn't think she could bear the silence that would fall between them if she did not.

'Plan to what?' Nicholas prompted.

'To . . . well, to do a lot to the cabin.'

'Yes. More coffee?'

'Please.'

She noticed that he was careful not to let his fingers touch hers when he gave back her mug. He remembered the raised knee and was keeping his distance. She smiled wryly at herself. No, it was not that. He wasn't frightened of her.

'I expect I look a mess,' she said ruefully.

'A little rumpled.'

There it was again, the unexpected kindness. Her eyelashes were matted, and her skin always blotched when she cried, but he merely said she looked rumpled. His kindness was disarming.

Oh hell, why couldn't he just be hard and nasty? She could cope with that. It was the kindness that had her confused. She did not know how to behave with him. She had planned to be dignified. Cool and aloof. But somehow his personality made that difficult.

'You know I've been crying,' she muttered after another of those silences.

'Yes.'

'You haven't asked me why.'

'I figured if you wanted to tell me, you'd do so.'

He was getting to her, he really was. 'Such a diplomat,' she scoffed. 'Such a saint.'

'Is that really what you think?'

'Yes!'

'I don't think you mean that.'

In a voice that was almost inaudible she said, 'No, I guess not.'

The tears were beginning to form again. They were pricking her eyes, and she could feel a tightness at the back of her throat. She should get out of the kitchen quickly, before she made a complete idiot of herself. She put down her mug and stood up. And knew she couldn't face going back to that awful bedroom.

She sat down again. 'I wouldn't believe it if you said you weren't curious.'

'I'm curious.'

'Then why haven't you asked me any questions?'

'When you're ready to talk, you will.'

Any moment she was going to cry. She rubbed the back of her hand across her eyes. She was so tired. So damn tired of everything. Of being alone. Of not being able to talk about what had happened. Of keeping up her guard. If Nicholas hadn't walked in, unwanted, uninvited, there'd be no guard to keep up.

She looked at him, scowling.

'Now what I have done?' She heard his amusement.

'Nothing,' she muttered. Fatigue was making her behave foolishly. All those tears, all the emotion . . .

She stood up again and went to the window. It was dark outside. The snow was still falling. Small flakes, soft small flakes. Amazing how they built up. By tomorrow the drifts would be even higher.

And Nicholas would still be here.

'A man tried to rape me.'

There. She had said it. Calmly, without expression. As if she was talking about something quite trivial.

Nicholas's breath came in a hiss. She heard it all the way across the kitchen. 'My God!'

'His name was Lance.'

'You don't have to talk about it if you don't want to,' he said tensely.

'They all said, "Talk. Tell us what happened".' It was hard to keep the tears from her voice. She rubbed furiously at her eyes.

'You don't have to . . .'

'Yes, I do. I don't know why, but I do.'

'Cathy . . .' She heard him coming up behind her. 'I had no idea . . .' He put his hands gently on her shoulders, only to withdraw them as she shuddered.

'I can't bear to be touched.'

'No . . . of course not. I'm sorry. I should have realised.'

He took a few steps away from her. She was glad he couldn't see her face. The tears were spilling on to her cheeks now.

After a while she said, 'I thought there were no tears left.'

'You can cry,' he said, very gently. And then, 'I don't have such a thing as a handkerchief. Will paper towel do?'

She actually managed a little laugh through her tears. 'You're a very kind man.'

'I'm not kind,' he said awkwardly.

'Yes you are. That's why I'm talking to you.'

After that it was still a while before she could go on. She dried her eyes with a piece of paper towel. The fire was burning low and Nicholas put on a new log. She watched him. Abstractedly she noted his hands, big and broad and competent. Such strong hands for a man who had such gentleness in him.

'You can talk some more tomorrow,' he suggested at length.

'No. I'll tell you now, while I have the courage.' She left the window and sat down in the chair by the fire.

'I was his student. I studied painting with him.' She looked at Nicholas. 'I don't know why I'm telling you all this. Anyway, you might have read about it in the papers.'

He shook his head. 'I don't go in for that kind of stuff very much. Sorry.'

'Oh, don't be sorry. I wish other people hadn't read it. It caused a minor scandal. Is there more coffee?'

'Sure,' Nicholas said, and refilled her cup.

She sat for a minute or two, silently, her hands around the hot mug, regaining some steadiness from the warmth. It was so tempting just to go on sitting in silence. Nicholas would not press her for details of the incident.

But she knew she had to talk. 'It was all so sordid,' she went on at last, her voice low. 'He was an attractive man, all the students were crazy about him. When he showed an interest in me I was flattered. We . . . we started to see each other. We met for coffee, we went to a show. All the time he wanted to make love to me, but I . . . something kept me back. He began to get impatient, aggressive. I began to get scared. I realised I couldn't handle the situation and I wanted to get out.'

'He couldn't accept it?'

'He threatened me. I did an assignment. Badly, because by then I was feeling so confused.' Her voice shook. 'He said he would fail me unless . . . unless I slept with him.'

'Bastard,' Nicholas said.

'Yes. Yes he was. We had a terrible argument. I said I would report him for sexual harassment. He lost his temper. One thing led to another. And then . . . he tried to rape me.'

'Tried?'

'My room-mate walked in just in time.'

There were a few moments of silence. Then Nicholas said, 'I don't know what to say.'

'It's all been said.' Cathy didn't know how bitter she sounded. 'I decided to lay a charge. There was a trial. Lance said my work had been deteriorating, that I was frightened of failing. That I'd offered him sex in return for passing grades.'

'He was believed?' Nicholas asked incredulously.

'He's such a personable man, and he made it sound so reasonable.' Cathy's voice shook. 'It was all so sordid. So incredibly sordid.'

'How did it end?'

'He was found guilty. But I didn't come out of it unscathed.' She looked at Nicholas. 'In the eyes of much of the world I was equally guilty. I thought at least my fellow students would understand. Some did, my friends . . . But there were people who believed that I must have led him on.'

'What a horrible experience.' Nicholas's expression was sober.

'First the attempted rape. Then the trial. I felt I had to get away. You found it strange that I'd want to be alone.'

'I didn't understand.'

'But you do now?' She looked at him and saw him

nod. 'When I saw the teahouse advertised it was like an answer to a prayer. My parents left me some money. Just enough to buy this place. As for the rest ... I have a children's book to illustrate, and I'm hoping to get some more commissions after that. And I'll paint. Perhaps my paintings will sell, and ...'

She broke off. 'You're frowning. You don't seem convinced.'

'What about people, Cathy? I know you're hurt, confused. But you can't live alone forever.'

'It's what I want,' she said stubbornly. 'I thought you'd understand.'

'I understand,' Nicholas said deliberately, 'that this is a place to lick your wounds. But afterwards—what?'

'There can be no afterwards.'

'There has to be.'

She got abruptly to her feet, some coffee spilling on to the floor as she did so. 'You're talking about men?'

Very quietly, he said, 'Yes.'

'I was attacked, Nicholas!'

'I know.'

'Obviously, you don't understand. You're not a woman, and you don't understand.'

'I'm trying. I know you've been hurt, shocked. I understand that you've been through an ordeal.'

'Well then?' she demanded, a note of hysteria entering her voice.

'Eventually you'll have to put it behind you. The idea of being a hermit might be tempting but it's not going to get you back to living with other people.'

'I've finished with other people. I don't trust them, I don't want them. For God's sake, don't you understand?'

'We're all sociable animals, Cathy.'

'Not me,' she denied violently. 'Have you any idea how I felt when I saw you yesterday?'

'I haven't forgotten the screwdriver, if that's what you mean,' he said drily.

'I would have used it.'

'You've been badly frightened, but the average man isn't a rapist, Cathy.'

'Maybe not.' Her voice dropped to a whisper. 'I can't even be touched.'

'Cathy . . .'

'You touch my hand and I feel violated. You kissed me today and I thought I would choke.'

'Lance has a lot to answer for.' There was a terrible anger in Nicholas's voice.

'He has,' Cathy said. 'Oh, he certainly has.'

Nicholas asked her if she wanted to sleep in the kitchen that night, but when she said no he made no protest. Instead he lit a fire for her in the bedroom.

'You won't need a chair against the door,' he said when they were saying good night.

She was actually able to smile. 'I guess not.'

He hesitated. 'Will there be nightmares?'

'I don't know.' She frowned. 'At first they came all the time. Every night, a few times every night. Lately there have been very few.'

'There was the one last night.'

'Yes.'

He looked at her. 'You were being attacked again?'

'There was a man trying to force himself on me.'

'Me?'

It was her turn to hesitate. 'I'm not sure. I guess the shock of finding a stranger here brought it on.'

'May I comfort you if I hear you scream?'

Her instinct was to say a blunt 'No.' Strangely, the words that came out were, 'I'd prefer it if you didn't.'

Something came and went in his eyes. A little gruffly, he said, 'Don't you know that I wouldn't hurt you?'

After a long moment she was able to say, 'I . . . I guess you wouldn't.'

They stood looking at each other for a long moment. Their eyes held, and Cathy saw the strength in Nicholas's face. Here was a man who was so sure of himself that perhaps he would not need to force a woman to his will for his gratification or in order to prove something to himself. Though she couldn't be sure of that—how could you ever be sure? For some reason she couldn't sustain the gaze, and she shifted her eyes before he did.

'Good night, Nicholas.'

Softly he said, 'Good night, Cathy.'

Breakfast the next day was the most relaxed meal they had shared. Cathy baked muffins from a packaged mix she had brought with her from Calgary, and Nicholas said they were so good that he would insist on getting the recipe so he could pass it on to the chef at the hotel.

She laughed at that. 'Flatterer.'

He pretended to look offended. 'Are you saying my taste isn't what it should be?'

'You said it, I didn't.'

'Bake them tomorrow and I'll have another go at test-tasting.'

'You mean you'll still be here by then?'

Nicholas went over the window and peered outside.

It was not snowing, but much had fallen during the night and the sky looked grey and swollen. 'I would think so.' He turned to her. 'Do you mind?'

Her answer came out easily. 'No.'

He looked at her, his eyes questioning. 'Will you miss me when I go?'

I really will miss him, she thought, surprised. 'I might,' she replied.

'From you that's a compliment.'

She decided to change the subject. 'Will you send hikers to visit me?'

'Will you serve them muffins and then insult their taste?'

'On the contrary, I'll flatter them and ask them to come back for more.'

'And will there be a muffin for me if I decide to walk up the trail?'

'On the house,' she answered him.

'In that case I'll give you all the free advertising I can manage.'

They laughed together, easily, happily. Cathy looked around her—at the cosy kitchen, shabby still but with clean walls and a sparkling floor; at the crackling fire and the remains of the muffins on the table between them, and she felt . . . comfortable.

'You look as if you slept well,' Nicholas said, almost as if he had read her thoughts.

'I did.'

'No nightmares?'

'Not one.'

'Good.'

She struggled with herself a moment. 'I suppose you know that I laid myself on the line last night? Telling you what happened?'

The smile vanished from his eyes. 'I'm glad you did.'

'I was scared.'

'Of what, Cathy?'

'Rejection, I guess. Disgust. Oh, I don't know . . .'

'Did you think I wouldn't believe your story?'

After a moment she said, 'There was that possibility.'

'You forget, I've come to know you.' He smiled as she gave him an incredulous look. 'Okay, so we've known each other barely two days, but we've been together all that time.'

'You don't really know anything about me,' she said slowly.

'Wrong. I know that you're a feisty lady.'

She laughed. 'The screwdriver again.'

He shook his head. 'Only a feisty person would tackle this place. You had no idea what you were coming to, but you took a chance.'

'Foolishly, I realise now. Without you I'd have been lost.'

'You might have had a tough time but you'd have managed.' He was silent a moment. 'I saw the way your shoulders drooped the first night, when you realised what a mess you'd come to. But you straightened and got to cleaning it up.'

'What are you trying to say, Nicholas?'

He looked at her, an odd expression in his eyes. 'That I would never doubt what you told me. And that I'd like to be your . . .' he hesitated a moment, then he said, 'friend.'

She felt something very strange stir inside her. She tried to ignore it because she knew it was something she couldn't accept.

'I'd like you to be my friend,' she said lightly.

'Cathy . . .'

His hand moved towards hers on the table. She saw it coming, and froze. For a moment she steeled herself not to react, and then she moved beyond his reach. Almost at the very same moment Nicholas withdrew his own hand.

'I'm sorry,' he said tensely.

'I can't.' Her voice was strangled.

'I'm sorry,' he said again. And then, in a more normal voice, 'What's on the agenda for today?'

At Nicholas's suggestion they made a start on the bedroom. True, Cathy's first concern had been the kitchen. But it was a lot cleaner now. There was still much to be done there but she would do it all in due time. Now Nicholas saw the bedroom as a priority. How she could sleep in that awful room was beyond his comprehension.

Together they scrubbed the walls and the floor, a chore that took them all morning. But it didn't seem too arduous, for they talked as they worked. Now that Cathy had spoken about herself, it was easy to talk, and the conversation was interesting.

She told him about her love of art, and the book she had been given to illustrate despite the scandal. About the projects she planned for the future.

And Nicholas told her about his career as a champion skier.

'Nicholas Perry,' Cathy said slowly. 'I knew I'd heard the name but I couldn't think where. You had an accident . . .'

'Which left me with my limp. I had to give up skiing, and I went into the hotel business instead.'

'A base for skiers. Does it bother you to see them go

out every day?' She put her hand over her mouth. 'I'm sorry, I shouldn't have asked that.'

'Nothing to be sorry about. It used to bother me, it doesn't any more. I've learned to live with it.'

'So you had your trauma too.' She was quiet a moment. 'I guess there's a lesson in it.'

'I think there is,' he said.

'I'm not ready for it.'

'One day you will be.' His voice was warm and kind.

'Perhaps . . .' In her own ears she didn't sound convinced.

'Yes,' he said with conviction.

After a moment she said, 'But I don't really think so, Nicholas. You see, it's not just the touching. I don't trust people any more.'

His face was hard. 'You can't live like this, Cathy. No physical contact. Always distrustful. Just because one man was a swine doesn't mean all others are the same. You have to take each man for what he is.'

'I don't intend to take any man at all.' Her expression was fierce.

'How long do you think you can go on like this?'

'Forever.'

'There's no such thing as forever,' Nicholas said. He took a step towards her.

The familiar panic started inside her. 'Nicholas, no!'

His face was etched with frustration but his voice was quiet. 'One day you will change your mind about things. And I hope I'll be around to see it.'

I hope so too, she thought without much hope. But she did not say the words aloud.

It was still snowing. Would it ever stop? Cathy wondered. She had never been truly snowed in before.

It was an eerie experience. She tried to open the front door but it wouldn't budge, and when she looked out of the living-room window she saw that the drifts reached half-way up the pane. But the back door opened, for the wind was not blowing that way. She stepped outside a few moments, her feet sinking deep in the snow, and enjoyed the luxury of the fresh cool air.

'This is something I've never experienced,' she said when she came back inside.

'It doesn't snow in Calgary?' Nicholas teased.

'You know what I mean. It snows, and sometimes it's pretty, and other times it's a darn nuisance. But by and large you can still get around. This . . .' She gestured. 'It's beautiful but I never imagined such isolation.'

'Still certain this is what you want?' He was watching her.

'Yes of course.'

'You'll be marooned here at times. Still sure you can take this kind of loneliness?'

A few days ago the answer would have been simple. Loneliness was what she had craved then. She had not distinguished it from solitude, had not analysed that the two did not mean the same thing. She wanted to be alone. Lonely, alone, private, isolated. The words didn't matter. They all had the same meaning. Or so she had thought. At any rate, she had known that what the words represented was what she wanted.

Now she was not quite so sure. She had got used to having Nicholas in the house. The sound of his voice, the smell of his pipe. A human presence. The cabin would seem very empty when he left.

'I wish you'd never come,' she said suddenly.

'What brought that on?' he asked mildly.

'Did you never stop to wonder if you'd be welcome?'

'I thought I was welcome—by now. Was I wrong?'

'Yes!' She swung around to look at him, and saw the understanding in his eyes. He *knew* how she felt. Darn him, he knew a damn sight too much about her.

'Why are you so angry, Cathy?'

'Because I was childish just now and I hate being childish.'

He grinned. 'We're all less than adult sometimes. That's not your only reason.'

'It isn't,' she agreed in a low voice. 'I do like having you here.' It was an admission she had never thought she would make.

'And you resent that?'

After a moment she said, 'Yes.'

'Why?'

'I think you know the answer to that.'

'Put it into words.'

'Nicholas Perry, psychiatrist,' she mocked. And then, 'I know I'm being unfair to you, that you're just trying to help me.' She pushed a hand through her hair. 'Okay then. I'm sorry that you've shown me what it would be like not to be alone.'

'Ah.' His lips had lifted at the corners and his eyes were warm. 'The first step.'

'No, Nicholas. It doesn't mean that I'll pack up and go back to Calgary. I'm as determined as ever to make a go of life up here.'

'You don't have to prove anything,' he said. 'To others, to yourself.'

'You still don't understand.' Frustration edged her voice. 'I am never going back to the life I had. People mean hurt, and I've done with hurting. I want to be alone. I just . . . well, it may take me a little longer than I thought to get used to it.'

'And if you don't?'

'I will,' she said in a voice that she hoped defied further argument. 'I'd like to make a start on the living-room today.'

'Without me.' Nicholas took his pipe from his pocket and began to light it.

'You're leaving?' She didn't hear the disappointment in her voice.

'No. But the cleaning will keep. Let's give it a break for today, Cathy.'

'You don't have to work. It's not your cabin, and . . .'

'Stop being so darned uptight. Did you think I was going to sit back and watch you work? I want you to give it a break too, Cathy. Let's relax together.'

Together. A strong word, she decided shakily. There had been togetherness in these days they had shared. They had worked together, talked together, eaten together. Slept beneath the same roof together. And now they could relax together.

It was going to become more and more difficult to see Nicholas leave.

'What do you suggest?' she asked lightly.

'Do you play Scrabble?'

'I love it. Don't tell me the Mortons left us a set.'

She wasn't aware that she had used the word 'us'. She didn't see Nicholas smile quietly to himself.

'Actually, I thought I'd make one.'

'How?'

Airily he said, 'There's a piece of old cardboard in the kitchen, I've been keeping it for just that purpose. It will make a splendid Scrabble board. And bits of paper will do fine for the letters.'

She laughed. 'You have an inventive streak.'

'And you have a lovely laugh—did you know that?'

The laughter wavered on her lips. 'Nicholas . . .'

'Just an observation,' he said quietly.

'A personal observation.'

'You can handle it, Cathy.'

After a moment she said, 'I guess I can.' What she didn't tell him was that since Lance she had been utterly unable to handle personal remarks of any kind.

The game was hilarious. Nicholas complained that Cathy knew more words than he did, that she was using words the longest dictionary wouldn't include. Cathy replied that Nicholas had compiled the board according to his own ideas, with scant regard for the rules. They bickered and they laughed, and now and then they interrupted their game just to talk. Cathy won, but Nicholas said they would have to have a return match and then he would give her a real run for her money.

'Was that more fun than scrubbing walls?' he asked while they were waiting for the kettle to boil.

'More fun than I've had in as long as I can remember,' she told him spontaneously.

'I'm glad.'

She was caught by something in his tone. She looked at him. Warmth and seriousness mingled in his eyes. And something else. An expression that made her feel weak.

The laughter vanished suddenly from her eyes. 'Why don't we get the board ready for the next game?' Her voice was jerky.

'There's something else I'd rather do.'

There was no mistaking his meaning. Fear leapt inside her. She tried to push past him as he closed the gap between them and put his arms around her. Instinctively she lifted her knee.

'Don't,' he said. 'There's no need for that.'

'Then let go.' Her voice shook but she lowered her leg without making contact.

'I'm not going to hurt you, Cathy.'

'You know how I feel, Nicholas.' She was a little desperate.

'Yes, I know.' His lips moved against her hair.

'I can't bear to be touched.'

'That's why I'm touching you, dearest.'

She heard the endearment but she didn't even try to make sense of it. All she knew was that she was being held against her will and that every nerve was rebelling in protest. Had the man been anyone else she would have had no qualms about hurting him. But this was Nicholas. And so . . . so there *was* a difference . . .

'Why are you doing this?' she demanded.

'Relax,' he whispered.

His body was long and hard, and though he held her loosely she was aware of every inch of it. 'I hate it,' she burst out in a choked voice.

'I want you to enjoy it.'

'I can't!'

'I want to see that you do,' he said.

And she realised, despairingly, that he meant it.

CHAPTER FIVE

'WHY?' she managed to get out at last.

'Because you can't go on like this.'

'I'm happy as I am.'

'I don't believe it. You're a lovely woman, Cathy. Don't make yourself a hermit.'

His arms were hard and muscled, and his body felt warm even through the clothes that separated them. As the scent of sensual maleness touched Cathy's nostrils, memories surfaced. Memories of a time when she'd taken pleasure in a man's caresses. And then she thought of Lance, and that memory drowned out the others.

She struggled against Nicholas. 'No! Let me go. Please!'

She was shaking. Her legs were so weak that if he hadn't been holding her she might have fallen. Nausea was building up at the back of her throat, and her temples were pounding. But he didn't let her go. She brought her fists up between his chest and hers, and pushed as hard as she could. 'Let me go, damn you!'

'Let me show you how good it can be.'

He was so gentle, so tender. If he'd forced himself on her, she could have fought it. It was his tenderness that she couldn't handle.

She gave a little sob of despair. 'You don't understand.'

'I'm trying. You've been hurt, Cathy, badly hurt. And now you've gone into hiding.'

'What of it!'

'You're hiding from the world. From yourself.'

'This is where I want to be.'

'The scars will fade.'

'You know nothing about it!' she shouted.

His lips moved in her hair. 'I do know that you can't shut yourself off from life.'

'This isn't life.' She pushed her hands against his chest, hard, and wondered if he had felt it at all. 'This is just . . . sex . . . pawing.'

He began to run his hands along her back. And it was awful. There was the nausea, and the trembling. The wish to be free of him.

And then suddenly, added to the sick sensations, she was aware of a burning where his fingers touched. Excitement. The first real physical excitement she had experienced since Lance.

She cried out, 'No!' And wasn't sure if the protest was directed at Nicholas or at herself.

He mistook the reason for her distress. 'I'm not going to hurt you.'

'I hate it,' she sobbed.

He held her a little away from him then. Cupping her face with his hands he looked down into eyes that were wide with shock. His own face was troubled. 'By now you must know that I wouldn't hurt you?'

'Yes . . .'

'Then what is it?'

'The memories.' She was shivering violently.

'They'll go with time.'

She shook her head. 'They'll never go.'

'I'll see that they do.' And when she shook her head again, 'For heaven's sake, Cathy, you can't go through life with a screwdriver and a lifted knee.'

'Why not?' Her throat was so dry that it was hard to speak.

'You're building a wall around yourself. It's not healthy to shut yourself away from people.'

'At least I'll never be hurt again.'

'And you'll never know love or friendship.'

'That's just fine.'

'What about marriage? Children? All the things women want?'

'Not this woman,' she said fiercely. 'Leave me alone, Nicholas. I'm a lost cause, don't you understand? God, I keep dreaming that the snow has gone. I'd like to wake up and find you gone.'

'Well, don't you feel good and sorry for yourself?'

Her head snapped back in shock. This was the contemptuous Nicholas she had met the first day. Nothing gentle in him now.

'Maybe I do,' she jeered back. 'With good cause.'

'Poor Cathy. Traumatised and humiliated. Life ruined.'

She felt tears pricking behind her eyelids, but she knew she wasn't going to cry. She was far too angry.

'You don't know the first thing about it!' she shouted.

'So tell me.'

'I've told you. Now take your filthy hands off me.'

He dropped them. 'Poor Cathy,' he said again. 'Twenty-three years old. All alone on a mountain-top for the rest of her life.'

'I hate you!' she hurled at him.

'Hate away.'

She strode away from him. At the window she pressed her face against the cold pane and took a few long deep breaths. At last she asked, 'Why are you doing this?'

'You tell me.'

'You think I'm weak. Stupid.'

'I remember saying you were a feisty lady.'

'Obviously you didn't mean it.'

'You know better than that.' Some of the mockery had left his tone.

She couldn't face him. Not yet. She went on standing at the window, her eyes fixed on the snowy vista. But she didn't actually see the mountains and the trees and the grey sky. She was too aware of Nicholas, just a few feet away from her, to concentrate on anything else.

She did not have to see him to know how he looked. Somehow he had imprinted himself on her mind, so that every feature was as clear to her as if she were looking at her own mirror image. The widely spaced eyes, deep blue and intelligent. The lips, firm yet sensuous. The firm jaw, the high cheek-bones. The long hard body. He was no more attractive than other men, she tried to tell herself. And all the time she knew she was not being honest—he was the most dynamic man she had ever met.

Why did I have to meet him now, *after* Lance? she wondered.

'I know what you're trying to do,' she said at last, her voice pitched very low.

'That's something.'

'You're trying to help me, but you don't understand that it's too late.'

'I don't believe that.'

'I wish you would.'

'No,' he said, coming up behind her. 'I don't want you to believe it either.'

'There's no help for me, Nicholas,' she said with returning fierceness.

'You *are* feeling sorry for yourself.'

'That's not true!'

'Then why won't you let me try to help you?'

She was so frightened. So terribly frightened. A strange sort of fear. Different from the fear she'd experienced that first afternoon, when Nicholas had been a stranger sitting in her kitchen. Then she had had the benefit of a self-defence class and a screwdriver, and she had felt reasonably confident of her ability to defend herself.

But the fear had changed. She felt as if she had entered uncharted territory, where the nature of her fear was not clearly mapped out, and where she had no idea how to look after herself.

'Look at me,' he urged softly.

'I . . . don't want to.'

'Please, Cathy.'

She wasn't sure why—but she did turn then. She was trembling. But as he took a few steps towards her she didn't move away.

'I want to touch you,' he said.

'I . . . I'd rather you didn't.'

'Just a touch. Nothing more.' He put his hand, very lightly, on her cheek. 'There, that's not too bad, is it?'

She shook her head, unable to speak.

For what seemed a long while his hand rested on her cheek, not moving, not caressing. Nicholas was so close to her. She could see the thick lashes that framed his eyes, and the tiny lines that ran together to make a cleft in his cheeks. She dropped her own eyes, and was sorry she did so. For she saw the long taut legs and the slim hips, and suddenly there was a heat in her groin that she had never thought to feel again.

'My God!' she thought, appalled.

'I'm going to touch the rest of your face.' He spoke softly, slowly, as if to a child.

But there was nothing child-like in Cathy's reactions as the long fingers began to trace a path around her eyes, and then her nose, and lastly around her mouth. She closed her eyes, so that Nicholas would not be able to see the tumult of emotions that raged inside her.

'Did Lance hurt you very much?' Nicholas asked.

She felt as if she was choking. But she managed to say with some semblance of calm. 'No. He didn't have a chance. I was lucky in that, I suppose . . .'

'I see.'

'It was the outrage.' It was very difficult to talk about Lance with Nicholas so close to her, touching her. 'But it could have been so much worse.'

'Thank God it wasn't.'

'It was bad enough. The treachery. The malice afterwards. The way he turned things back against me at the trial.'

Nicholas stroked her hair. 'He was obviously the worst kind of bastard. But I'm glad he didn't hurt you too much physically.'

Her eyes snapped wide open. 'Are you taking his side?'

'Of course not. But if he'd hurt you really badly then the trauma might have been even worse. This way—well, I'm hoping you'll get over it more quickly.'

'There are some things a woman never gets over,' Cathy said sharply.

And she knew that it wasn't quite true. Not any more. She didn't want Nicholas to touch her, but at the same time she felt a mounting excitement. And she hated herself for being so—was the word 'weak'? She didn't know. She did know that she was not prepared to tolerate the new sensations. She had come here to find peace of mind. The very last thing she wanted was new confusion.

His fingers were exploring the area around her mouth once more. And then one finger was touching her lips. Cathy stood rigid as the finger traced the line first of the top lip, then of the full bottom one. Shock began to course through her as it slid between the two lips to the moist flesh in between.

It was too much! She jerked away from Nicholas. 'No!' The word came out as a shout, though she hadn't meant it to.

'I went too far.' Remorse was written all over his face.

'A damn sight too far!'

'You were so still. I thought perhaps you were enjoying it.'

'I was hating it.' Her eyes were smudged with shock and her face was white. 'It's no good, Nicholas. I can't go on with this.'

'Not right now, I can see that.' His eyes were bleak.

'Never.'

'You'll feel better about it tomorrow.' He seemed troubled, as if he realised that by going too far he had made matters worse.

'No.' She took a few steps away from him. 'It's no good.'

'You're a normal human being, Cathy. You need to be touched. We all need it.'

'Get your touching somewhere else!'

His lips tightened. 'We're not talking about me.'

'I don't need a seduction routine, Nicholas. Oh, it's different from Lance's, I grant you that. But you're a man, all you want is a bit of fun. Even if it's with a girl who's frigid.'

'Stop this, Cathy.'

But she couldn't stop. She knew that what she was saying was ugly, perhaps even untrue. But she couldn't seem to stop.

'I don't need a noble knight—if that's what you really are. Keep away from me, Nicholas. It's all I ask.'

'You're very foolish.' His face was hard now, as if he was fast losing patience with her. 'But if that's the way you want it, that's how it will be.'

Nicholas walked out of the kitchen, leaving Cathy alone. She could hear him in the living-room. She wondered what he was doing but she had no intention of going after him. Perhaps she had said too much, perhaps she had misjudged him, but no way was she going to apologise.

Restlessly she paced the kitchen. Emotions churned inside her, like a flooding dam about to break its walls. She was so overwrought that she felt as if she would explode. Filling a pail with water, she began to clean the stove, sloshing the water every which way, attacking the shabby old surface with unnecessary violence.

All through the police interviews and the consultations with lawyers, she had tried to keep her emotions in check. The trial had been nasty but she had managed to live through it. She had coped with the slurs and the gossip which followed the ordeal. She had tried very hard to turn herself into a kind of robot, a mechanical being who went through all the correct motions, a doll with no feelings of her own beneath the shell. What kept her going was the resolve that no person would have the power to hurt her or affect her again. If ever she felt upset or unhappy or rejected, only she herself would know about it. Nobody would be allowed to see beneath the outer shell again. And till today, by and large, she had not done too badly.

But in just a few minutes everything had changed. And she didn't know if the new world she had so carefully created for herself would ever be the same again.

Damn Nicholas! What had possessed him to touch her like that? Didn't he understand that touching was no longer part of her life? Never could be? And as for herself, why had she submitted? She should have pushed him away the moment she'd understood what was happening.

Why hadn't she done so?

The answer was both appalling and unacceptable. For it involved her reactions to Nicholas. She could have pushed him away so easily. But she had chosen not to do so. And now she was paying the price.

Just a few minutes of sensuousness had been enough to shatter her. To seduce her. For, yes, Nicholas had seduced her senses with those clever fingers of his, and she had let him do it. Oh, what she would not give to erase the memory of those few minutes! Savagely she pushed her hand through her hair, as if the gesture could achieve what she so desired. But she knew it was useless. Nicholas had touched her, and she had responded. It did not matter that he did not know it. What mattered was that she knew it.

At first she had been repelled by his touch. But gradually excitement had taken over. Her skin had tingled beneath his fingers, and there had been the heat in her groin which she had never thought to feel again. Her mind had waged war with her body. While her mind had rejected what Nicholas was doing, her body had willed him to do more. That was what she could not accept.

Until today she had been convinced that she would never let a man touch her again. She'd been so sure that the sexual side of her nature had died with Lance's attack. She'd been so sure that she wanted to live alone, that there could never again be a relationship with a man. And then Nicholas had explored her face with his fingers, and now the only thing she was sure of was that she was very far from being the aloof unfeeling girl she had hoped to become.

Nicholas had shown her that she possessed a sexuality which was more potent than she had ever suspected.

She got up suddenly, knocking over the pail in her hurry. She barely noticed the soapy water spilling over the floor she'd waxed with such loving care. All she knew was that the walls were bearing in on her. Three days were too long to be cooped up in a cabin without a breath of fresh air and in the company of too virile a man. She had to get out.

Nicholas was still in the living-room when Cathy pulled on parka and boots and made for the kitchen door. She had to push against the door, but at least on this side of the house the drifts were not so high that she could not get the door open. She stepped out, sinking down into the snow which engulfed her all the way to her knees.

The air was like chilled champagne—effervescent, sparkling—and Cathy took deep greedy gulps of it before ploughing forwards. All around her were the mountains, mysterious and brooding. The snowy landscape was beautiful in a hushed, haunted way. But the scenery didn't impinge on her consciousness. She could think only of Nicholas and of the astounding demands of her own treacherous body.

With the snow so deep the going was hard. Each step was an undertaking. But Cathy was undeterred. Her breath began to come in gasps, and her thighs ached with the effort it took to move forward, but she went on all the same. She was putting distance between Nicholas and herself, and that made the effort worthwhile.

She could not rid herself of the scene in the kitchen. She wanted only to forget it, yet it was replayed over and over again in her mind. Nicholas's exploration of her face. The way his hand had moved on her skin. The feel of his fingers beneath her eyes, their taste on her tongue. Her revulsion, her feeling of panic at the thought that her privacy was being violated once again.

And then there were those other sensations. The ones which more than anything she wanted to forget, though she knew already that she would remember them a long time. The inexplicable seduction of her senses. Her growing excitement. The need, the totally abhorrent need, to feel the long male body closer to her own.

If Nicholas had set out to prove that she was still a

woman who needed warmth and tenderness and touching, he had succeeded beyond anything he could have imagined. His sensuousness had shown her a degree of sexuality which she had never suspected. Even before Lance she had never felt quite so aroused.

'How could you, Nicholas?' she asked aloud in a voice choked with frustration and unhappiness. She could have been so happy in the teahouse. There would have been enough to satisfy her. The beauty of the mountains, her illustrating work, her collection of record albums. But Nicholas had insisted on showing her another, deeper, side of herself. She recognised with despair that her own company might never be quite enough for her again. And there was not a thing she could do about it.

She did not know how far she went. It was only gradually that she realised how cold it was. It was also much darker than when she had set out. It was time to go back.

Which proved to be easier said than done. She turned the way she'd come—this was the way she'd come, surely?—and was confused when she didn't see the cabin. She looked first in one direction, then in another—and all she saw was snow. Could she have walked so far without knowing it?

But hey, her tracks. She had only to follow her tracks and she would be right back at the cabin. Optimism came—then went. The wind had risen, blowing snow across her tracks. In something of a panic she stumbled over territory that was unfamiliar to her. The snow seemed suddenly deeper than before, the effort to push her way through it was greater. And she was so cold, so terribly cold. After a few steps she stopped—for, no, the cabin did not seem to be in that direction. She went another way, only to stop again. The wind was blowing the snow in her face now, stinging her cheeks, blinding her eyes. It seemed to get colder and colder. Her face and her toes and her fingers were beginning to feel numb.

She had no idea where the cabin was. It was as simple as that. The wind and the snow and the gathering darkness had combined to make her disorientated. I'm going to die here, she thought.

It was then that she heard the first shouts. 'Cathy! Cathy! Cathy, where are you?'

'Help! Nicholas, help!' she shouted back.

'Where are you?'

'Here,' she responded. Only to realise that she couldn't tell him where 'here' was. 'I don't know. . . .'

'Stay put,' he shouted. 'I'll get to you.'

He called to her constantly, and she answered. The sound of her voice led him to her. By the time he reached her she was so cold that it was an effort to speak.

One look at her was enough. He took off his woollen toque and drew it over her head. He knotted his scarf around her throat, then wound the long ends of it around her face.

'Can you walk?' he asked urgently.

She could only nod.

'Walk in my footsteps,' he ordered, his tone rough and angry.

He seemed to know just where to walk, and she followed him. She did not care that he was angry. She was beyond thought, beyond emotion. Keeping her legs moving, first the one leg then the other through that thick deep snow, that was the only reality.

The cabin seemed to come at them quite suddenly through the twilight. A light was on and smoke was rising from the chimney. Tears pricked suddenly at Cathy's eyes, and just then the last of her strength gave out.

Nicholas, glancing behind him, was just in time to see her crumple. She heard him exclaim as he reached for her. He lifted her in his arms and carried her inside.

'Thanks,' she gasped.

'You little fool,' he bit out harshly.

She was beyond coping with his anger. She said, 'I . . .'

But he cut her off. 'Skip it. Whatever you think you have to say, just skip it.' She was still in his arms, and he was looking around for a place to put her. Finally he just put her down, quite gently, on a chair.

'Are you okay?'

She nodded. She could not talk. She was trembling, and her teeth were chattering so loudly that the sound seemed to fill the room.

'No you're not,' Nicholas said savagely. 'You're freezing. A little longer out there and you'd have had hypothermia.'

She was too cold to argue the point. Every Canadian knew about hypothermia. It could cause irreversible brain damage, and without immediate help the condition was fatal.

'Can you take off your mittens?' Nicholas asked.

He watched as she struggled vainly for a few moments. Then he was bending over her, drawing the mittens from her cold hands. He studied them closely for signs of frostbite, then held them between the palms of his own hands to give them warmth.

He knelt down to take off her boots. As Cathy flinched, his glance flicked up and she saw that he was still very angry.

'Don't go coy on me.' His lips were tight. 'You know damn well that we have to get your things off. And you seem in no state to do it.'

He was right of course. She knew she should be grateful to him so she did not resist him further. He held her cold feet in his hands and then he put his palms against her face. Such big palms they were, they covered a good deal of surface.

She was still trembling. If anything, her body was shaking more violently than before.

'You're really freezing,' he said at last.

'I feel as if I'll never be warm again.'

'Oh yes, you will be,' he said grimly. 'I'll see to that.'

She managed a weak smile. 'You're a very determined man.'

'Better believe it. Not that you deserve it after the damn-fool stunt you pulled.'

'You're so angry, Nicholas.'

'Believe that too. I touch you and you go sprinting off into the snow. Why?'

There was no way she could answer that. Not now. Perhaps never.

Fortunately he didn't seem to expect an answer. He had gone to the stove and put on the kettle. 'Bed's the only place for you,' he said when he came back to her.

'I don't have one.'

'You don't, do you. But you do have a sleeping-bag. I'll bring it in here.'

'I'll be okay in the bedroom,' she protested, immediately disturbed.

'You're going coy on me again. And I'm in no mood to humour you.' He frowned down at her. 'You'll lie right here where it's warm. Good God, Cathy, don't you understand that you could have died?'

Once more he didn't wait for an answer. He strode out of the kitchen, returning moments later with the sleeping-bag. 'It's not much warmer than outdoors in that room,' he said feelingly.

She watched him lay the sleeping-bag on the floor. She was about get into it when he stopped her.

'Get those clothes off first.'

The breath jerked in her throat. 'No!' And then, 'Why?'

'You know the reason.' He put his hand on her jeans. 'Stiff with cold. And that shirt you're wearing isn't much better. Off with them, Cathy.'

Her lips were dry. 'I'll change in the bedroom.'

'You're not leaving this kitchen.'

One look at his face was enough to tell her that any argument would be wasted. And her clothes were cold and hard and uncomfortable, he was right about that. 'At least—turn the other way.'

He gave a short laugh. 'You take this aloofness thing too far. If you could see what you look like—a small scared icy waif—you'd realise you were in no danger of being molested.'

'Nicholas, you know I can't . . .'

Unexpectedly his lips lifted, and his eyes held the ghost of a smile. 'I'll turn my back if it will make it easier. But be quick about it.'

Nicholas went to the stove, and Cathy began to take off her jeans and shirt. Briefly she thought of asking him to fetch a change of clothes from the bedroom but she discarded the idea. The request would only call forth another angry remark. She wasn't wearing a bra and so she had on only a pair of bikini briefs when she slipped into the sleeping-bag.

'Decent?' Nicholas asked. His back was still to her but she heard the laughter in his voice.

'Yes.'

'Good.' He came to her carrying a mug with steam rising from it. 'You look snug enough. And here's some tea to warm you up.'

Tea! Just what she wanted. Then she remembered. There was no way she would sit up, shirtless, braless, in front of Nicholas. 'I don't think I can manage it.'

'You're too cold to sit up?' He frowned, then his expression cleared. 'I'll help you.'

He knelt beside her. Supporting her head with one hand, he brought spoonfuls of tea to her lips with the other. Tea had never tasted so good. Something else was good too. The feeling of being cared for and cherished.

I could get used to this very easily, Cathy thought.

But this was not the time to harden herself against the idea. She was weak and dizzy with fatigue, and her body still trembled with cold. Nicholas fed her slowly, allowing for time between one hot spoonful and the next. He seemed to have infinite patience, this ruggedly attractive man.

'Still cold?' he asked at last.

She managed a weak smile. 'Better.'

'Your face is white and I see a shivering body in that sleeping-bag.' He grinned. 'What makes you so stoic?'

'I'll warm up soon,' she said.

'Sooner—with some help.'

For a moment she did not know what he meant.

Disbelievingly she watched as he took off his clothes. He moved so quickly that by the time she understood what he was doing it was too late to resist. Her trembling increased a hundredfold as the warm naked male body slid into the sleeping-bag with her.

'No!' She was in a state of shock as she tried to get out.

'Yes.' His arms went around her, holding her to him.

'Get out, Nicholas!' Her breath came in a sob. 'Oh God, Nicholas, you can't. I won't let you!'

She was trembling so violently that Nicholas was reminded of a wild bird beating itself to death against the bars of a cage. He was filled with an overwhelming compassion for this shocked, frightened girl.

'I'm not going to hurt you. Cathy, I'm not going to hurt you.'

Her voice was choked with tears. 'Get out!'

'I will, darling, the moment you're warm.'

Why did he call her 'darling'? Was it just another trick? 'I'm warm,' she said.

'You're frozen. And this is the best way I know to warm you.'

It took a while for Cathy to grow calm. The last man to be so close to her had been Lance. Every nerve seemed to rebel against this new closeness. Nicholas was so big, so strong, he could overpower her with very little trouble at all. The screwdriver was with her things in the bedroom, and in the state she was in she doubted that her self-defence techniques would be very effective.

But Nicholas had no intention of hurting her. He did not mean to take advantage of her weak state in order to overpower her. Finally she understood that.

The sleeping-bag was very small, meant only for one person, and so Nicholas was very close to her. His arms were around her, but he lay quite still. He was giving her warmth, and that was all.

Well, not quite all. It was only as Cathy's breathing slowed, and the warmth began to return to her frozen body, that she began to understand the strain Nicholas was under. His breath was on her neck and in her ears, and it had a harsh sound to it. The hands that held her were still but there was tension in the arms. The long body was taut and hard and throbbing.

Nicholas was a man aroused, but for all that he was keeping himself under amazing control. It had to be very difficult for him, Cathy acknowledged, but not with word or action was he telling her how he felt or what he desired. Under similar circumstances Lance would have cracked a long time ago.

Nicholas was not Lance. Nor did Cathy's feelings for Nicholas in any way compare to her feelings for Lance. It was time that she admitted it to herself.

CHAPTER SIX

'I'M sorry,' Cathy said at last.

'You should be.'

He desired her, but he didn't sound in the least lover-like. What Nicholas didn't know was that Cathy was beginning to suffer a strain similar to his own. As the terrible coldness left her she became acutely aware of him. Just the touch of his hands on her face had been enough to send her out in the snow. But this— this lying together, two naked bodies in the confines of a sleeping-bag made for one—was like nothing she had ever dreamed of.

Far from being cold, she was burning. They were so close together that their bodies were touching, from their feet all the way up to their necks. Cathy lay with her back turned to Nicholas but she did not need to see him to know how he looked. She could feel him, smell him. She seemed to be *part* of him. The sensations she'd felt earlier in the day were surfacing again. Excitement, the gnawing ache in her groin.

If Nicholas were to make love to her now, she doubted that she would be able to resist him. Part of her wanted him more than she had ever wanted anything in her life. But there was a part of her that was still wary and fearful.

'I suppose you're wondering why I did it,' she said in a small voice.

'I think I know why. It was because I touched you.'

His breath fanned her cheek, and his hands were warm on the bare skin beneath her breasts.

'Yes.'

'And now I'm touching you again.'

'Yes . . .'

She could feel every one of the long fingers burning her skin. She was filled with a sudden longing to feel his fingers on her breasts. She wanted to guide them to where she wanted them to be. But something— shyness, insecurity—held her back.

'Did you really hate it so much?' Nicholas asked.

She was silent a while. Could she tell him how mixed-up she felt? Did she want to?

'Can't you tell me?' he asked.

The sensuousness of their situation made it hard to tell him anything. He must have been uncomfortable, for he moved slightly, and as she felt him against her, hard and throbbing, the most alarming sensations shot through her.

'I was frightened,' she said, when she could speak.

'I tried to be gentle.'

'I know . . .'

'Surely you didn't imagine it was all leading up to another rape.' His voice was harsh.

'No. I knew you wouldn't hurt me.'

'Then what was it, Cathy?' When she remained silent, he added, 'It must have been pretty serious to send you rushing out into the snow like that.'

Would he never let up? No, Cathy thought, he would not. He felt entitled to an answer and he would go on questioning till he had it. Even then, she did not have to give in to him. But she had a sudden need to be open with him. It was not something she had to think about, it just happened.

'I was frightened of myself,' she admitted.

She felt him tense against her. 'Want to talk about it?'

She gave a little laugh that was more like a sob. 'Like this? It's the darndest way to talk, Nicholas.'

'Meaning you don't want to.'

'Right—but I guess I've reached the point where I have to. I didn't understand what I was feeling, Nicholas.'

'Try to tell me.'

If she told him, she would be telling him what she was feeling again now. The excitement, the uncertainty. The longing, and the fears that went with it.

So softly that Nicholas had to strain to hear her, she said, 'I thought I never wanted to be touched again. I was so sure.'

'And you discovered you were wrong?'

'I think so. Nicholas, I'm so confused.'

'Are you saying you want me to make love to you?' His tone was soft now.

'I don't know.'

Which was not entirely true. She ached to turn to him, to feel her breasts against him, to twine her legs with his, to taste his lips. She had not known what it could be like to want a man so much. But the fear was still there, and the uncertainty. She wanted him to make love to her, and yet she was terribly frightened of what would happen if he did.

'You must know how I feel right now.' Nicholas's voice was urgent. His body was rigid with tension.

'I do,' she whispered. 'Oh Nicholas, I'm sorry I'm putting you through this.'

'I sense I could persuade you to let me make love to you.'

'Perhaps. I don't know. Nicholas, I just don't know.'

'You're going to have to make up your own mind.' The harshness was back but she realised that it was occasioned by strain. 'You have to be ready for it.'

'Yes . . .'

'In the meanwhile I'm going out of my mind.' He pushed himself away from her. 'You seem warm enough now, Cathy. You don't need me any longer. Not for this kind of warmth anyway. And I'm a normal man. I don't know how much longer I can control myself.'

He climbed out of the sleeping-bag. Cathy watched him walk across the kitchen to pick up his clothes, naked and proud, magnificently built and superbly the master of his own needs and emotions. He was right about one thing, the bone-chilling coldness was gone. She was no longer in danger of any after-effects from her escapade. What Nicholas didn't know—though perhaps he had guessed—was that she was disappointed and frustrated. On her own she had not been ready to say 'Yes, please make love to me.' But she sensed that she would have needed little persuasion.

'You're different from Lance,' she said suddenly.

He looked up from buckling his belt. 'I should hope so.'

'I couldn't have blamed you if you'd . . . well, if you'd tried to persuade me. Lance had no control at all.'

He grinned at her but she noticed that his eyes were serious. 'I hope that's not the only point on which I differ from Lance.'

'You're not like him in any way,' she said, and with a sudden lifting of the heart she knew that it was true.

'I think we're making progress,' he said softly.

She was filled with sudden joy. 'I think we are.'

She was warm now. She was also hungry. 'I'm coming out,' she said.

'Good.'

'Turn your back, will you, Nicholas?'

His eyes were filled with laughter. 'I could just about draw every inch of your body.'

'I still want you to turn your back.'

She was neither uptight nor tense. Just a little shy. And Nicholas, bless him, didn't argue the point. All he said was, 'Will you cook us some supper?'

'Of course.'

'Then I'm prepared to turn the other way.'

She was out of the sleeping-bag and putting on the clean clothes he had brought her after he had got dressed, when she said, 'Lance didn't have much of a sense of humour.'

'Poor guy. I hope that's something else we don't have in common.'

'You know it is. Things might have been different if he'd had some lightness in him.'

He turned to look at her, his expression compassionate. 'You will stop thinking about him, you know.'

'I'll never forget.'

'You'll think about him less and less.'

She was able to meet his eyes. 'I think I'm beginning to know that now.'

And she was able to laugh with him as they planned their supper menu. 'The choice is enormous,' she informed him. Canned lasagne, canned frankfurters, canned tuna, canned chicken. Mashed potatoes and canned vegetables. Not till the snow melted and the pack-horses could make their way up the trail would Cathy be able to stock her freezer with fresh meat, fruit and vegetables. They settled on lasagne with peas and stewed tomatoes, and were still laughing as they sat down to eat a candle-lit meal.

The tension of the day could have continued to mount. Instead, something seemed to have been settled between Cathy and Nicholas, so that they were able to relax and enjoy each other's company.

Nicholas raised a glass of tomato juice in a toast, and as Cathy toasted him back she felt a tightening in her throat. He was so attractive in the flickering light of the candles. His eyes were deep and mysterious, and his lips curved at the corners in a smile that still lingered from their last joke. The lines of his face were softened but even now he looked tough and rugged. Yet I know that he can be gentle and tender, Cathy thought. And fast upon that thought came another, 'Do other women know it too?' She pushed the question away, for it hurt too much to think about it.

Later, when they'd washed the dishes, they came back to the table. Their conversation centred on the cabin, on the chores they might tackle the next day. Cathy hoped she was making the correct responses but her real thoughts were elsewhere.

'You look a thousand miles away,' Nicholas commented at length.

'Actually my thoughts were right here in this cabin.'

'What are you thinking about?'

'You. Me.'

Something flickered in his eyes. 'I like the sound of that.'

Quickly she said, 'Without you I wouldn't have learned that I could live again.'

'You know that now?'

'Yes.'

'I want to teach you to trust. And to love.' He reached his hand towards hers across the table, tentatively, giving her time to withdraw if she wanted to do so.

But she didn't withdraw her hand. A little breathlessly she said, 'Maybe . . .'

His hand covered hers then, the big rough hand folding over the small smooth one. A quiver shot through Cathy but a small one this time. For how long would that first touch be difficult?

'Does it bother you?' he asked.

She looked at him, hesitantly, beneath her lashes. 'No.'

For at least a minute he kept his hand quite still. Cathy was the first one to move. She let her fingers curl around his hand, so that she was holding him too. It was her first response. She darted another look at Nicholas and saw that his eyes were on her face. He knows how I feel, she thought. He knows me so well. Oddly the fact did not disturb her.

Another half minute passed. Then Nicholas began to move his thumb. Slowly, over the back of Cathy's hand, and then along the wrist, first the outside of the wrist, only afterwards on the sensitive blue-veined area below her palm. If the movements were slow, they were also sensuous. Cathy felt excitement building inside her, mounting, burning, till it became an effort to sit quietly.

'Is that too much for you?' Nicholas asked.

She was honest with him. 'I'm enjoying it.'

His breath was coming faster. The game they were playing was exciting him too, but he seemed determined to take it at her pace. 'Do you think you're ready for more?'

She wanted him to kiss her. 'I'm wondering—does your beard scratch?'

'I kissed you once,' he said huskily.

'And I pushed you away ... *Does* it scratch, Nicholas?'

He laughed unsteadily. 'You don't expect me to answer that. It's something you have to find out for yourself.'

'I do, don't I.'

'Witch!'

He got to his feet, drawing her up with him. He was a good eight inches taller than she, but she tilted her face up towards him. He cupped her face in his hands, his fingers sliding beneath her hair, his thumbs at the base of her neck. He didn't kiss her immediately. He just looked down at her, and she looked back at him, frightened still, but wanting him more than she feared him. Something in her eyes must have given him the answer he needed, because he bent his head to her then.

He began to kiss her, tentatively at first. His lips brushed her cheeks and her eyes and the sensitive area beneath her ears. She stood quite still, just inches away from him, letting him kiss her where he pleased, wanting to respond, yet not quite able to give herself permission to do so. He lifted his head and looked down at her, and she saw his expression, fevered yet questioning. He was waiting for her to tell him what she wanted.

'It tickles a little,' she said.

'And how does that feel?'

'Nice.'

'Cathy . . .'

'Nicholas, I . . .'

'I don't know what you want. And I don't want to frighten you.' There was an odd sort of urgency in his tone.

'I want . . .' She hesitated. 'I want to know how your beard tastes.'

As he drew her against him she could feel the laughter moving in his chest. And then he was kissing her again. Her lips this time. Light kisses still, as if even now he was wary of frightening her. But such sensuous kisses, tantalising, so that in moments warmth spread through her whole system. The response she had been denying herself came automatically now. As she felt the tip of his tongue tease the corners of her mouth she opened her lips to him. Her body, suddenly on fire, arched against him.

He lifted his head again. 'Cathy . . .?'

She darted him a look that was party shy, partly mischievous. 'So now I know how the beard tastes.'

'And does it please you?'

'Very much.' Her look was bolder now. 'What I'm trying to say is . . . I like it when you kiss me.'

As they came together again, his kisses became more passionate. Deep and hungry, searching, and finding too, for Cathy was finally responding. His tongue explored the sweet moistness of her mouth, and after a few moments her own tongue came to meet it. His hands moved over her, sliding over her back, shaping themselves to her waist, her hips. And then he touched her breasts.

Cathy gasped and grew rigid. The last man who had touched her had been Lance. And Lance had shocked her, outraged her. Now she was being touched again.

For a moment she didn't think she could accept this new man's hand on her body.

And then it came to her—Nicholas was not Lance. His caresses were as different from Lance's as day was from night. She'd had to fight Lance. She could *enjoy* Nicholas.

Nicholas had grown motionless. His hand still hovered near Cathy's breast but it was as if he was waiting for some sign from her to tell him what she wanted. Suddenly Cathy knew what she wanted. She put one of her hands over his and guided it back to her breast. And then she wound her arms around his neck and buried her fingers in his hair.

The blood was pounding in her head and she was filled with a wild joy. She had crossed a hurdle. She had been so frightened but she had crossed it. And now she knew what it was she wanted. What she had been wanting earlier in the day, before her headlong dash into the snow.

She did not stop Nicholas as he began to unbutton her shirt. She *wanted* him to kiss her, to touch her. A part of her was shocked with the depths of her need, but another part was wildly elated. The girl who had intended to spend the rest of her life in seclusion now wanted this man to find her beautiful, desirable.

Tenderly, almost as if he was worshipping her, Nicholas caressed her breasts, exploring the soft curves, teasing the nipples till they swelled and hardened into the palms of his hands. And then his lips followed where his hands had been, setting off such a tumult of emotion inside Cathy that she gave a small moan of pleasure.

She was consumed with sensation now. Her limbs were weak and the blood was singing in her veins. But even then, on the periphery of her mind, she was registering Nicholas's contained passion. He was so close to her that she could feel his arousal, but he was considering her all the way.

Nicholas was the first to draw away. She looked up at him confused, her eyes dazed with passion, her lips parted. 'Nicholas . . .?'

'If we go on now I won't be able to stop.' His voice was husky.

'No . . .'

'I'm not sure that you're ready for more.'

She hadn't even considered the inevitable next step. All she knew was that she wanted him to go on kissing and caressing her. 'I don't know . . .'

'I want you to be ready. I don't think you are—yet.' He buttoned her shirt. 'It's best this way.'

He was right of course. She wasn't ready. She'd thought they could go on kissing and touching, she'd forgotten they were adults and that there could be only one conclusion. And she didn't know if, when the time came, she'd have been able to go through with it. Nicholas was right, she wasn't ready.

She was also disappointed. Frustrated. A frustration which she knew Nicholas shared.

Without looking at him she said, 'Yes, it's best.'

They kept her sleeping-bag in the kitchen that night. Nicholas said Cathy couldn't possibly go back to the bedroom, and she needed little persuading. The thought of sleeping in that cold bleak room was daunting.

Cathy watched Nicholas get ready for the night. There were the two armchairs pushed together, the parka that did duty for a blanket. It seemed incredible that the long body could get any measure of rest on the improvised bed.

'You can't be comfortable like that,' she said ruefully.

His eyes gleamed. 'Can you think of something better?'

She hesitated, torn between wanting and not wanting to rise to the unspoken suggestion. If Nicholas were to share the sleeping-bag with her there could be only one ending to the night. But before she had made up her mind what to say, he shot her a lopsided grin. 'I guess people have had to make do with less.'

It was fortunate that the Mortons had also left some old clothes in the cabin, for without them Nicholas would have had to wear the same things day after day. He had washed a couple of shirts and a pair of jeans, faded and shabby the lot of them, and left them to dry, and now he had a change of clothes when he needed them. Mostly, Cathy realised, he wore them at night.

She watched as he took off his shirt, her eyes moving with pleasure over the superb body, the broad shoulders, the narrow waist, the muscled chest and back. In the firelight his skin was like burnished copper. He must have felt Cathy's eyes on him, for he turned and looked at her, and as their eyes met she felt an increasingly familiar sensation burning inside her. Oh, but he was an attractive man. Physically the most attractive man she had ever met.

But was that all there was to his appeal? Physical attractiveness? A sexual spark that kindled some answering spark inside herself? Or was there more to what she was beginning to feel about him?

Mr Morton's old clothes were too small for

Nicholas, the shirt sleeves too short at the wrists, the jeans too short at the ankles, but it didn't seem to bother him. For the first time she realised that she had taken for granted his ability to cope without the most essential necessities.

'What do you do about a tooth-brush?' she asked curiously.

'Had one with me.'

'You mean you knew there was going to be a blizzard? That you'd be stranded?'

'What a suspicious mind you have,' he said, but affectionately. 'I mean that I always carry certain things with me.'

'You're a survivor,' she said slowly.

'I guess I am.' He turned to look at her. 'And it's what I want you to be.'

'I am,' she said tersely. 'You keep saying I'm feisty.'

'You're that all right. But I was talking of something else.' And they both knew what that something was.

As he knelt beside her and ruffled her hair he was grinning once more. 'Good night, Cathy.'

'Nicholas . . .' She stopped, not quite knowing what she wanted to say. Confused, because there were things she could not seem to put into words.

But he seemed to understand. His lips touched hers, gently, with none of the passion of the lover an hour earlier. 'Sleep well,' he said softly.

An hour later she was still awake. The fire was burning low, throwing soft shadows on the walls and the newly waxed floor. Nicholas was asleep, his long body looking awkward and yet at the same time strangely relaxed on the chairs. Cathy lay in her

sleeping-bag and listened to the sound of his steady
breathing.

How different this was from the nights spent alone
in the dreary bedroom. The kitchen was warm and
cheerful. But the greatest warmth came from the
presence of the sleeping man. It could not go on
snowing much longer. Soon Nicholas would go back
to the hotel, and she would miss him more than she
had ever imagined possible.

Which brought her back to the question she had not
answered for herself earlier. What made Nicholas so
appealing? Was it just a physical thing? A matter of
the right chemistry between two people?

Or was there something more?

No idle question. 'I want you to be ready,' Nicholas
had said earlier. It was what she wanted too. But would
she know when she was ready? How would she know?
For a young woman of twenty-three the answer should
have been relatively simple. But since Lance nothing
had been simple. Once Cathy had been resolute and
outgoing, eager to face life, to make friends, to have a
career. But since the trauma with Lance her enthusiasm
had been replaced with fear and uncertainty.

The reason she had refused to sleep with Lance was
because her principles had never allowed for casual
sex. It was not so much that she felt she had to be
married to a man before she could sleep with him as
that she had to know she loved him. Much as she had
enjoyed Lance's attention, her deeper feelings had
never been touched. There had been other men she
had liked, not one she had loved.

Perhaps I don't know what love is, she thought with
sudden despair. Would I recognise it if it happened to
me?

Her eyes grew heavy, and in rhythm with the steady breathing of the sleeping man, her own breathing began to slow, and she fell asleep at last. She dreamed that night about Nicholas. Not a nightmare this time. She and Nicholas were walking beside a lake, and in a clearing they stopped and Nicholas began to make love to her. And Cathy responded, eagerly, happily.

Her lips were curved in a smile when she awoke. In the half-conscious state between dreaming and consciousness her mind was still filled with the pleasure of the lovemaking. In a way it was the only thing that was real.

It was at least half a minute before she understood that she was not by a lake but in the kitchen of a snow-bound cabin. And then she became aware of certain sounds and she knew what had woken her. Opening her eyes, she saw that Nicholas was papering the walls.

Absorbed in his work, he did not notice that she was awake. And she did not tell him. She lay in her sleeping-bag and watched him. Part of one wall was already papered and he was busy pasting another strip. Not without a certain amount of effort, she saw, realising that with her help the task would have been much easier. More pleasant too, especially for Nicholas, who, she remembered, had told her that wallpapering was not one of his favourite pastimes.

So why was he doing it? To surprise her. To please her. The answers came to her through a burst of happiness. Nicholas was doing something he disliked because he wanted to give her pleasure. She continued to lie there watching him, enjoying the long lean look of him, the tilt of the proud head, the way he pursed his lips as he whistled softly to himself. She could have lain there all day just watching him.

At length she said softly, 'Hi.'

The whistling stopped as Nicholas turned. 'Good morning.' He finished smoothing down the paper, then came to her. 'Lazy-bones. What time is this for a decent woman to wake up?'

'Catching up on my beauty sleep.'

He bent over her to drop a kiss, feather-light, on her forehead. 'I've no quarrel with that—you do look beautiful. I like you like this, with your cheeks all rosy'—he kissed first the one cheek then the other—'and your hair a mess.' He wound a strand of it round his fingers.

She smiled, warmed by his teasing. 'It's a treat to see a man up and about while a woman takes her leisure.' And then, 'Didn't you say you hated wallpapering?'

'*I* said that? How does it look, Cathy?'

'Great! I can't wait to see the whole kitchen done. I'll help you do the rest.'

'I won't say no to that,' Nicholas said feelingly. 'Nor would I say no to some breakfast.'

Unexpectedly she wanted to say, 'Make love to me. Please, make love to me.' She was filled with a feeling that was altogether new, and somehow precious. But it happened so suddenly, and it startled her, so that she wasn't altogether sure what it meant. She did know that she wanted to savour it for a while.

And so she just said, 'Do muffins sound good?'

'Excellent. The coffee's ready.'

She did not tell him to turn away as she climbed out of her sleeping-bag. She was almost naked, and his eyes were on her, but she did not mind. She saw his gaze on her long slender legs, on her waist, on breasts that had hardened beneath his touch last night—and she felt tremors of sensation shivering through her. God, how she wanted him. But she could wait. For she knew now that they would make love.

After a shower and a change of clothes, she came back into the kitchen and opened another package of muffin mix. Nicholas was still wallpapering, talking and stopping to sip his coffee as he worked.

This could so easily become habit, Cathy thought, enjoying the comfortable intimacy. It was not the first time the idea had occurred to her but never before had it been quite so poignant. There was a kind of rightness in this kitchen. Togetherness. A sense of sharing.

'The sun is shining,' she remarked idly.

'No snow since last night. I'd say the storm has passed, Cathy.'

Disappointment hit her. And a kind of grief.

'The drifts must still be quite high,' she said carefully.

'Yes. But another day or two and I should be able to make my way down.'

'I see . . .'

He was watching her. 'You wanted to see me gone.'

'That was a few days ago.'

'Things have changed?' He was smiling just a little. Abstractedly Cathy noticed that the smile made a cleft which ran from his eyes to the corners of his mouth.

'You know they have,' she whispered.

He took a step towards her. 'Cathy?'

'Yes,' she said fiercely, 'I'll miss you. Isn't that what you wanted to hear?'

They had breakfast together, and afterwards they worked together. And all the while they talked. Nicholas told Cathy more about his days as a skier.

Till now he had not gone deeply into the subject, perhaps because it hurt too much, and Cathy was conscious that on his side too there was a deepening of trust and feeling. In other circumstances the knowledge would have thrilled her, she knew. But not now. She could think only of the lovely togetherness that was about to end, just when it had come to mean so much to her.

'Something wrong?' Nicholas asked once.

'No.'

He tugged at a strand of hair before pushing it back over her forehead. 'You look sad.'

She gave a strained smile. 'I'm not sad.'

Which was not true. This morning she'd woken with such a feeling of happiness. There had been the wonder of realising that she wanted Nicholas to make love to her. It hadn't mattered when it would be, she had known it would happen in the fullness of time.

And now time was running out on them.

All day they worked in the kitchen and by evening the room had undergone a transformation. But Cathy hardly noticed it. Wallpaper and decorations were not as important as they had been on the day she had arrived.

'Feel like playing Scrabble?' Nicholas asked after supper.

'I don't think so.'

'There *is* something wrong. You've been so quiet all day.'

She was trembling. 'I thought you'd know . . .'

'Something I've done?'

For a perceptive man he was being unusually obtuse. Or perhaps it was just that he wanted her to

make the first move. She got up from her chair and
went to him. 'Will you kiss me, Nicholas?'

He stared up at her tensely. 'Cathy . . .?'

She put her hands on his shoulders. 'Make love to
me, Nicholas. Please make love to me.'

CHAPTER SEVEN

NICHOLAS'S head jerked back. 'Cathy?'

'Make love to me.' Her voice was jerky with nervousness.

He sat very still, his long body suddenly taut. 'Is that what you want?'

His head was on a level with her breast, his closeness was setting off tiny fires inside her. 'You said I should be ready. Nicholas—don't you want to?'

'I've wanted nothing else for days.' His arms went around her waist as he pulled her on to his lap. 'I just want to know that you're sure.'

'I'm sure.'

'No regrets later.' His voice was unsteady, moving her, because she saw the depths of his own need.

'No regrets,' she whispered.

A hand went to her chin, tilting it, bringing her face close to his so that he could see into her eyes. It was as if he was seeing into the very core of her being, she thought with a shiver of excitement. And then the same hand slid to the back of her neck, cupping her head, so that he could kiss her.

It was a kiss that was unlike the others. Slower, deeper—hinting at secrets to be shared, promises to be kept. Just at the beginning, when her body was captive in the circle of his arms and his tongue played inside her lips, there was the familiar stirring of panic. Cathy shuddered, habit urging her to push herself away from this man, instinct warning her to escape while she still could. But within moments the tremor of fear became a shiver of delight, and the panic was drowned in a flood of sheer sexual excitement. Lance was forgotten—there was only Nicholas.

His lips and his tongue brushed the soft skin of her throat, lingered in the little hollow where the pulse beat a crazy tattoo, then moved upwards to play around the corners of her mouth and beneath her eyes. Cathy's eyes were closed, she did not know that she was moaning with pleasure. Nicholas's kisses were a seduction of the senses, so that she was conscious of nothing but the lips and tongue which seemed to move with a life and will of their own.

It was excitement that drove her into taking an active part. Without even thinking of what she was doing, her hands groped for his head, and then she was guiding him till her mouth met his. Their kisses became more frantic, with teeth and tongues meeting and caressing and exploring in an explosion of hunger and pleasure. 'You're so sexy, so lovely,' he said hoarsely, his lips moving on hers, his breath warming her mouth, so that she felt the words rather than heard them. And she knew that she had never felt more alive, more female.

One of Nicholas's hands went to the top of her shirt, brushing aside the collar so that he could caress the soft skin of her shoulders. Tentatively, as if even now he was waiting to see if she would push him away, he began to undo buttons. But Cathy had long since passed the stage where she could push him away, where she even wanted to do so. In her loins there raged a fire that needed to be assuaged, and her limbs felt weak with the strength of a desire that was stronger than anything she had ever imagined.

A hand cupped one of her breasts, a finger stroked a nipple that was swelling and hardening to the touch. Cathy closed her eyes. Somewhere in the hidden recesses of her mind was the knowledge that perhaps things were moving too quickly, but it was a fact she did not want to acknowledge. There was too much pleasure in the things Nicholas was doing to her. He caressed the other breast, then his lips touched the places where his fingers had been, and Cathy did not resist him. Small moans of pleasure escaped her lips as her body became a mass of achingly sensuous sensation.

She began to touch him too. All day she had been wanting to touch him, to know how his skin felt beneath her fingers. It was her turn to undo buttons, and even through her excitement she registered the accelerated pace of his breathing. Then his chest was bare and exposed, and she was revelling in the feel of hard lines and muscles, in the sheer strength and masculinity of him.

With a little movement he slid an arm beneath her legs, and then he was on his feet, lifting her up with him. For a long moment he supported her weight while he kissed her, her feet suspended some inches above the floor, her body against his. It was all so erotic that Cathy felt wildly excited. It was a few moments before new feelings began to surface— fragility at first and then vulnerability. It was this last which, even now, she could not accept. And so, though her mouth never left his, she made herself heavy, forcing him to let her stand on the floor.

Nicholas did not seem to register the show of independence, or perhaps it was just that he did not understand it for what it was. He held her a little away from him so that he could look at her. In his eyes was a look of something akin to worship, and his expression was tormented. 'You're so beautiful,' he groaned. 'The most beautiful woman in the world.'

He began to undress her, drawing the unbuttoned shirt from her shoulders, slipping off her jeans. She stiffened just for a moment when his hands were at her jeans, but then she relaxed. And when she understood that it was what he wanted her to do, she undressed him likewise. It was what *she* wanted too, though still, at the very back of her mind, almost as if it wished to be denied, was the fear that things were going too fast for her.

His arms went around her as he moulded her to him, the long hard lines fitting against the soft yielding ones, all the while his hands moving on her bare skin, over her back and along her waist, over her hips and lingering on the smooth rounded buttocks. Cathy let him do whatever he wanted because it was what she wanted too, and all the while her own hands were learning and exploring the shape and texture of his body.

'You're driving me out of my mind,' he said at last, lifting his head to look down at her. 'I suppose you know that?'

She met his gaze. 'Yes.'

'There's not even a bed.' His eyes went to the sleeping-bag. 'But there was room in there for two yesterday.'

There would be enough room anywhere for two people who wanted to be together. She watched him kneel to unzip the bag so that it lay flat and open. Still kneeling, he held out his arms to her, and she went to him willingly. He held her for some moments, caressing her, kissing her, just as he had done before, only with much more urgency now.

She couldn't have said quite when she began to be really scared. Later, when she thought about it, it seemed as if it started when they lay clasped together and she knew that she would soon be giving up something of herself.

Finally Nicholas could no longer control his need. He rolled Cathy on to her back and slipped a leg between hers. And then he was moving over her, his body coming down on hers. It was then that Cathy jerked, her whole body convulsed with fear, terrible fear. In that instant Nicholas was forgotten. The male body pressing down on hers was Lance. He was a man, any man, and he was using his greater strength to take from her what he wanted.

No! She tried to get the word out. No! No! But her throat was dry and constricted, and no sound emerged. She began to struggle wildly against him.

Nicholas went rigid. 'What's wrong?'

'No!' Sound had returned to her vocal cords. 'Get off!'

'Relax, darling. Please relax. We both want this.'

The endearment meant nothing to her. All she knew was that she had to get away from the big naked male body. She felt choked, trapped, violated.

'Cathy . . .'

Instinct and training came to mind at that moment. She was about to react in the way she'd been taught when he understood what was happening and rolled away just in time.

'Hell!' Nicholas lay on his back and swore.

Beside him Cathy was trembling violently, her hands over her eyes. Tears choked her throat. She was trying hard not to cry, but without success. The adrenalin that had given her strength moments ago was subsiding. Now all she felt was grief. She began to weep.

Nicholas made no move to comfort her. If until now he had been patience itself, at this moment he was six feet and two inches of angry frustrated male, with problems and emotions of his own to deal with. He sat up at length, and pushed himself away from Cathy who was still sobbing quietly. She dropped her hands to look at him through tear-washed eyes.

'I'm sorry.'

'Sorry!'

He began to dress, his movements quick and angry. Cathy did not want to watch him but she found she couldn't help herself. She felt sick to the very pit of her stomach.

'I really am sorry,' she whispered again when he was dressed and moving away from her across the kitchen.

He turned and looked down at her, a small crumpled figure on the ground. 'Like to tell me what that was about?'

She did not answer right away. She couldn't. She was still naked. That had not mattered when Nicholas had caressed her. If anything, she had been proud of her body. But now, in the unhappy aftermath of shattered expectations, she felt embarrassed and acutely self-conscious of her nudity. Eyes averted from him, she pulled the sleeping-bag around her.

'You've every right to be angry,' she muttered at last.

'Well, that's something.' He looked at her curiously. 'Would you really have crippled me?'

'I don't know,' she said after a moment, and knew that she wasn't telling the truth. At the height of her despair she would have done whatever was necessary to defend herself. The remorse—because Nicholas would not have deserved the punishment—would have come later.

Nicholas's expression was bleak. 'You started this, Cathy.'

Her voice was small. 'I know.'

'Last night, when I called a halt, it was because I knew there could be no stopping.'

She was so upset, she was hurting. But he was hurting too, which was why he was pouring salt in wounds that were already too raw. And she knew there was nothing she could do to stop him. He really did have a right to be angry.

'It was your idea to start this today,' he accused again coldly.

'Oh Nicholas, I know. Do you think I don't know? That I'm not bitterly ashamed?'

The unhappiness in her voice got through to him. For the first time there was some compassion in his expression. 'Cathy, why?'

It was so hard to talk. She needed time to be alone. Time to think, to come to terms with what had happened. How could she possibly explain it to him when even to herself she couldn't make sense of her conflicting emotions?

'Well?' Nicholas prompted.

She shook her head. 'I don't think I can talk about it.'

'Try.'

A little sob escaped her lips. Then she said, 'I thought I wanted you to make love to me. I thought I was ready . . . I really did . . . Oh God, Nicholas, I didn't mean to hurt you. But then . . .' She covered her eyes again. 'I'm sorry. I don't know what else to say.'

'You couldn't have thought I was going to rape you.'

'I don't know how to explain.' Her voice sounded as if it might break. 'At the time . . . Nicholas, all I could see was Lance.' She stopped, biting on her lip and blinking hard. At last, when she had herself a little more under control, she went on. 'I don't suppose you understand.'

He looked down at her without speaking, his expression difficult to read. After a moment he went to the window. Cathy watched as he stood there looking out into the night. His shoulders had never looked so square, his body so tense and rigid. What was he thinking?

After a while he turned. Something was on his mind, she could tell by his face. For some reason she began to tremble again.

'I do understand,' he said at last. 'I'd be insensitive if I didn't.'

'You were never insensitive,' she said in a low voice.

'It doesn't mean I can live with it.'

Something jerked inside her. 'What do you mean?'

'We can't go on like this, you and I.'

'You mean . . . you'd force me?' she got out the words.

'Don't be silly. What I mean is that it's becoming impossible for me to go on living this way with you. This tiny cabin. The isolation. I'm aware of you every moment, and I believe you are of me. It's driving us both crazy.'

Every word he said made sense. She wished that she didn't have such a feeling of impending doom.

'I'm a normal man, Cathy. I think you know what it

does to me, being with you all the time, seeing you, wanting you—because I do want you—and not being able to do anything about it.'

'I'm sorry,' she whispered on a dry throat. How many times had she apologised?

'I'm sorry too.' He sounded gruff. 'Because, in spite of all that's happened, I believe you're a warm passionate woman and that you're denying yourself something you really want.'

'I can't,' she said numbly. 'That's been proved.'

'Nothing's been proved,' he countered crisply.

'But it has.' She was nauseous with despair.

'I don't believe you are giving yourself a fair chance—not mentally, not physically.'

'I tried.'

'Yes,' he said softly. 'You did try.'

There were things she wanted to say, only she didn't know how to say them. Nor did she think Nicholas was in a mood to hear them. The time for talking was past. There was only one thing Nicholas wanted now, and that was to put some distance between them.

She looked at him where he stood across the room from her. There had been times when she had been struck by his gentleness. Now she could see only his strength, his innate maleness. She was still in her sleeping-bag, and from her vantage point he looked taller than ever, and so aloof. It seemed incredible that such a short while ago they had been wrapped in a warm, wonderful intimacy. She had felt that she knew him—the shape of his body beneath her fingers, the rippling of muscles, the thickness of hair, the feel of high cheek-bones, the taste of his lips. Yet now she did not know him at all. In the time that it had taken for him to put on his clothes he had become a stranger. A stern, remote stranger.

She tried to speak, but her mouth was dry. She licked her lips, and drew a deep breath of courage. At last she was able to get out the words, 'What will you do?'

'I'm going to leave.'

'Now?' The word sounded choked.

'In the morning.'

She swallowed hard. 'What about the snow?'

'I'll manage.' He looked at her, the lines of his mouth softening, as if he had some inkling of the way she was feeling. 'Remember, we talked about it earlier.'

'Yes. It's just . . .' She was unable to go on.

It's just that I feel as if you're abandoning me, was what she wanted to say. But he would think her crazy.

'Just?' he prompted.

'Well, there's still so much snow on the ground.'

'I'll be careful.'

'Nicholas . . . Nicholas, why not wait one more day?'

The look he gave her was bleak. 'It's best this way, Cathy. I think you know that.'

She did know it, of course. She had been playing for time, that was all, but twenty-four more hours in his company would do nothing to solve her problems. She just wished that she didn't feel quite so unhappy.

It was Nicholas who spent that night in the bedroom. He was absolutely adamant about it. After what had happened they both knew that they could not sleep together in the kitchen, for each would be too aware of the other. Emotions would be raw, there would be no peace for either of them.

'I'll sleep in the bedroom,' Cathy said.

But Nicholas would not hear of it. He was the one who could no longer tolerate the situation.

'Besides,' he said with a wry smile, 'tomorrow night I'll be back in my own bed.' Well, Cathy thought as she lay in her sleeping-bag on the floor of the dark kitchen, there was no peace for her this way either. In the end she had not been able to accept Nicholas's lovemaking. So now she was alone, as she had wanted to be from the moment she'd arrived at the teahouse. She should be calm and asleep. Yet all she could think of was Nicholas. She could see him stretched out on the two chairs, dressed in Mr Morton's old clothes and covered with his parka, and she wondered if he was sleeping. Or was he too awake?

Perversely, she longed to go to him. Which was of course out of the question. She had encouraged him once today, with disastrous results. She could not tempt him again.

'I don't know what I want!' she exclaimed suddenly, fiercely, in the darkness. 'Lance, what did you do to me?'

Nicholas had aroused in her emotions and sensations she had thought never to feel again, so that for a while she had begun to think she was over Lance, over the attack. But in the end what Nicholas had made her feel had not been enough. She knew now that she was not over Lance. Perhaps she never would be.

Nicholas waited till the sun was up, and then he went. At the door of the cabin he grinned down at Cathy. 'Take care, feisty lady.' He kissed her, very lightly, on the lips, and then he was gone.

She stood at the open door and watched him go, a

tall lithe figure, broad-shouldered and confident, making his way through the snow, his boots leaving great indentations as he went. He would be all right, she knew. He understood these mountains, this trail, and though there was still snow on the ground, Nicholas was the kind of man who knew how to look after himself.

Would she see him again? Yes, of course she would. The question was—when? The next question was—did it matter? The first question was easy to answer. She would see him in the summer, when he came up to the cabin for muffins and tea or when she took the trail down to the hotel. The second question was harder. Yes, it mattered. How much? Not too much, she tried to tell herself.

Only when Nicholas had vanished through the trees did she become conscious of the cold air seeping through the open door of the cabin. She closed it with a determined bang, then stood in the kitchen and looked around her. Despite the fire, the kitchen seemed desolate and forlorn. A little like Cathy herself. There was a void inside her, and at this moment she was not sure how she was going to fill it. She had not slept much last night and now she felt drained.

I'm going to miss him, she thought.

And yet it really had been time for him to go. They couldn't have gone on much longer as they were, he had been right about that. Since last night, when she'd drawn back from their lovemaking, the atmosphere had been charged with emotional tension. It was as if they had been living on a volcano which might erupt at any moment.

She went to the stove and put on the kettle. And she

felt the emptiness of the cabin close in on her. All
around her were memories of Nicholas, and she
couldn't escape them. The fire he had laid, the old
clothes he had worn and then discarded. The chair he
had always seemed to sit on. On the counter was the
Scrabble set he had made, beside it was the book he'd
been reading the day she arrived. There were several
rooms in the cabin but they had done all their living in
the kitchen.

I'm going to miss him, she thought again, and felt
her throat tighten. This would never do! 'It wasn't as
if I was in love with him,' she said into the oppressive
silence. Yes, she had grown used to having him
around, had enjoyed his companionship. But that was
all there was to it. That there could be more was
something she refused even to consider.

It was odd to remember now how frightened of him
she had been at the beginning. The screwdriver and
the nightmare. All of it only a few days ago, but it was
as if she had lived a lifetime in those few days.
Nicholas had become her friend. Almost he had
become her lover.

Almost . . . A pulse leaped in her throat. Nicholas
could never be more than a friend. She had thought,
she had really thought, that he could be more than
that, but it wasn't to be. And that was why it was good
that he had gone. The only solution. Nicholas was her
friend. But he was also a man and she was a woman,
and if they had remained together longer the volcano
might well have exploded with who knew what
consequences. She thought of Lance and shivered.

Abruptly she pushed the thought from her. She
couldn't go on like this. She really couldn't. She had
bought the teahouse because she wanted to make a

new life for herself. She remembered her first glimpse
of it through the trees after Larry had dropped her in
the snow. It had seemed a haven then, a new
beginning. It was still a haven now, it had to be.
Nothing had changed. Not really. Okay, there had
been a man in her life, and his going had left a void.
But that was only temporary. She was a feisty lady,
wasn't she? Wasn't she? She would get over it.

Starting now.

There was still lots to do before the teahouse would
be ready to welcome its first guests. In the days before
Cathy had left Calgary she'd had so many plans for the
place. She had had a picture of it constantly in her
mind, one that changed as her ideas for it changed. It
had been such fun to think, to plan. It had also been a
way to push Lance from her thoughts.

Somehow, since coming here the plans had grown
less clear. She knew why, of course. First there had
been the shock of finding a man in the cabin and the
knowledge that she had to defend herself against him.
And afterwards there had been the turmoil of her
changing emotions.

Now it was time to think of the teahouse again.

There was still so much to clean. Walls that needed
washing, floors to be scrubbed. And then wallpapering
and waxing. The kitchen was almost habitable now
but the other rooms were still a mess. And something
really had to be done about the furniture. It had
seemed like a bargain when she'd heard that the
Mortons had left all their furniture in the cabin. Some
bargain it had turned out to be! But until she had
money to buy new things she would have to make do
with what there was.

With thoughts of washing down the living-room

floor, Cathy filled a pail of soapy water. Only to look at it weakly. A moment later she'd poured the lot down the sink. Resolution was all very well, but if she didn't have some fun today she would be unutterably depressed.

She would make a start on the furniture. Now that *would* be fun. Creative. Challenging. Hopefully it would stop her dwelling on her loneliness.

Throwing all her energy into what she was doing, she began to sandpaper one of the kitchen chairs. There were six of them—wooden and highbacked with comfortable arm-rests. In a bygone time they had been a lovely walnut brown, but most of the paint had peeled away and they were shabby to say the least.

At last she was ready to paint. Once, in a magazine, she had seen something that caught her attention. Painted chairs with alpine flower motifs on the backs and arm-rests. They were lovely she'd thought at the time. She was going to create some of her own alpine chairs now. The first one would be an experiment.

The hours passed quickly as she sketched flowers on to sandpapered wood. Then, painstakingly, she began to paint them. Slowly the flowers that grew wild on the slopes of the Rockies in the summer came to life on the old wood. Cathy's back was aching by the time she stood upright to examine what she'd done, and her stomach told her it was time for lunch. She opened a can of tuna and ate it with crispbread. And when Nicholas came into her mind, she willed herself to concentrate on ideas for her art-work instead.

Lunch over, she painted the rest of the chair blue. And by the time the sun dipped behind the mountains and the light began to fade, one chair was ready. It looked wonderful—it was a success! Cathy looked at it and smiled. She would have six of these chairs in the kitchen. And a table that matched them. But that was only the beginning. Outside on the snow-covered patio, where hikers would sit in good weather, was a stack of weathered furniture. She would bring it in, a little at a time, and she would clean and oil the shabby wood.

At supper-time she wasn't really hungry, but she resisted the temptation to snack on the rest of the tuna and made herself a proper meal, just as she would have done if Nicholas were still here.

Still, as night closed in, it was hard not to think of him. She couldn't help wishing that he was here to see the chair, to hear her plans. To talk to her.

And yes—be honest—to touch her. Okay, so in the end she hadn't been able to go all the way and let him make love to her. But his caresses, his kisses, had been a joy. And no amount of telling herself anything else could change the way it had been.

It grew darker still, and Cathy was restless. She'd finished painting for the day, and it was too early to go to bed. She put another log on the fire, and then she went to the window and looked out into the night. If only she could see the lights of the hotel, then perhaps she wouldn't feel so isolated. She couldn't help wondering what Nicholas was doing. Had he gone to bed or was he regaling his friends with tales of the girl he'd met at the end of the trail?

Stop it! Stop thinking of Nicholas, she told herself, and wheeled savagely away from the window. Nicholas had his life, she had hers, and it was just as well that she couldn't see the lights of the hotel from here. There could be no bond between Nicholas and herself.

But she had a dream that night. Not the nightmare. Another dream like the last one, in which Nicholas made love to her. And when she woke up next morning, her pillow was wet.

CHAPTER EIGHT

CATHY opened the door of the cabin and went outside. Her boots left marks in the melting snow as she walked a little way along the trail, but she wore no toque, no mittens, and only a light parka over her shirt.

Spring had come to this part of the Rockies. Finally. The snow was melting, a little more each day. Every morning there were bigger patches of dark ground, soon the snow around the teahouse would be all gone. Only the high mountain reaches would still be white. It was just a matter of time before the slopes and meadows were green and dotted with wild flowers. Already a few squirrels were in evidence. Cathy smiled as she stopped to watch one scampering along the branches of a tree. There would be so many squirrels and chipmunks here soon.

Oh, but the air was delicious. After all the time spent in the musty cabin, the air seemed as effervescent as champagne, and she took deep breaths of it as she went. Each day she walked a little further along the trail. From where she was now she could actually see the cluster of buildings which made up the hotel. Red roofs glinting in the sun. Smoke rising. Tiny moving pinpricks that were people. Was one of them Nicholas?

The smile vanished from her face. She tried so hard not to think of Nicholas. Not always successfully. He popped into her mind at the strangest times, when she did not want him there at all. She would be painting a chair, or making a batch of muffins to freeze, and suddenly, there he would be. And she would find herself wondering what he was doing, wondering when she would see him again.

She did *not* want to think about Nicholas. But she thought about him anyway. Almost constantly.

She turned at length and made her way back to the cabin. On the patio she paused and looked about her with pride. The once-shabby outdoor furniture had been cleaned and oiled. On the cedar-logged walls were ceramic tiles which she had painted. Eventually each table would have a pottery vase with dried flowers. She had so many plans.

Today, with the use of the packaged mixes she had brought with her from Calgary, she was going to do some more baking. Very soon now the hikers would begin to arrive, and she meant to be ready for them.

In the cabin she looked around her again. Nicholas would not recognise the place, she often thought. Despite herself, she longed to show it off to him. The floral chairs in the kitchen, the wallpaper which he had started to put on and she had completed. The other rooms, clean and sweet-smelling now that the windows were no longer frozen shut and she could open them. Even the awful bedroom was habitable, though she was still using the sleeping-bag—she would never bring herself to use the bed. She'd get a new one eventually, but in the meanwhile the sleeping-bag was definitely her only option.

As she opened the cupboard and took out a package of muffin mix, she reflected on the way things had turned out. Just right really. With the cabin clean and bright it was the haven she had dreamed of in those unhappy days in Calgary. She had every reason to be happy.

'But I'm not happy.'

There! The words had been in her mind for days but this was the first time she'd said them aloud. It was not easy to admit to herself the one thing she had been trying so hard to ignore.

She was not happy. Well, and so what? Perhaps life at the teahouse was not quite what she'd hoped. It didn't mean she would throw it all up and go back to Calgary.

With hands that were suddenly jerky, she tore open the paper and threw the mix in a bowl. And then she stopped to wipe a floury hand across her eyes.

Nicholas had said she would be lonely. She hadn't wanted to believe him. But she *was* lonely. A strange kind of loneliness for a girl who had always enjoyed her own company. A loneliness that was making her restless, so that her mind was never quite on what she did. When she baked or scrubbed or painted, she would find herself reliving the days with Nicholas. When she was out of doors, the grandeur of the mountains did not keep her from looking towards the trail that Nicholas would have to take if he decided to visit her. It was a loneliness that was making her angry as well as restless, for she felt as if she was missing something. Nicholas had shown her a glimpse of something that could never be hers—and she did not want to miss it.

Could you want something and yet not want it?

It was at night, when she lay sleepless in her sleeping-bag, that she missed Nicholas the most. Restless, frustrated, she would find herself longing for him. Wanting him to caress her, to kiss her. Reliving the moments they had spent together. Remembering that she had asked him to make love to her because she'd wanted it so much. Remembering, too, how she'd pushed him away, because when the moment came she'd felt violated.

Which took her back to the question—*could* you want something and yet not want it? If only she could stop thinking about it, stop tormenting herself.

And then one day the first hikers arrived. Four young people, two girls and two men, with packs slung across their backs.

'Wow!' they said, looking around them in amazement. Evidently they had been here often in the past, for one of the girls said, 'Gee, I can't believe the change.' And one of the young men said, 'You've certainly done wonders for the place.'

They ate Cathy's muffins with obvious enjoyment, found it hard to believe that she hadn't made them from scratch, and insisted that she join them at their table. They were backpacking, they told her, and when she asked if they weren't cold at night on the still snowy ground, they laughed and said they had found ways of overcoming the problems, They were fun, these four, nice company. Cathy would have liked to tell them to stay longer, but eventually one of the young men looked at his watch and said that if they meant to get to their next destination before nightfall it was time to leave.

A little wistfully, Cathy watched them go. The sound of talk and laughter rang on the silent mountain air long after they had vanished from sight. As the last sounds faded, the loneliness closed in on Cathy again. If anything, she was more lonely than before.

More hikers arrived. They came singly or in groups,

sometimes just three or four in a day, sometimes more. They were easy people to please. Mostly they were so hungry and thirsty after their long climb that they were thrilled just to find a place where they could eat. The hikers brought news. News of the outside world. News of what was happening in Calgary and in Banff. News of the doings at Turquoise Lake Hotel. Cathy, who had no newspaper, no telephone, only a radio that was suffering from a case of bad reception, found herself craving news.

It was from a hiker called Todd that she learned about the ski championships.

'But the snow is drying up,' Cathy said, eyeing the ground around the teahouse.

'It is here. And the lower lakes are beginning to thaw. But it's still pretty deep at higher levels. Some places there'll be good skiing right through till April.'

'I guess you're right. And you say the championships are not far from here?'

'A couple of miles the other side of Turquoise Lake. Saturday and Sunday. Nick Perry from the hotel is one of the co-ordinators.'

It was strange to hear his name on a stranger's lips. 'Oh, is he?' Hard to sound casual.

'Say, why don't you come and watch?'

'There's the teahouse—I can't abandon it.'

Todd shook his head. 'I doubt you'll get people coming up here while the championships are on. Come along, Cathy, you'll have fun.'

'Maybe . . .'

It really was time she went down to the hotel to arrange about supplies. The trail was safe enough now for the pack-horses to bring up all the fresh things she was beginning to long for—milk and eggs, fruit and vegetables. There were also things she wanted Larry to drop from the helicopter. The day of the ski championships was a good time to go. The chance of disappointed customers would, as Todd said, be slight. And if, after concluding her business, Cathy decided to visit the ski slopes—well, what could be more natural?

On Saturday she took extra care with her appearance. She washed her hair and let it curl softly around her face. Beneath a ski-suit she wore a pretty angora sweater that brought out the green lights in her eyes. Make-up? She hesitated. Up here at the teahouse she rarely bothered with make-up. But today seemed different somehow. Her lashes were dark and long, needing no mascara, but she settled for a pearly green eyeshadow and a touch of bright lipstick.

In the woodshed she had found some old signs belonging to the Mortons. One pointed the way to the teahouse. Another said 'Closed today', and it was this latter sign which she took with her as she headed towards the trail.

It was a good day to be walking. Here and there the path was slippery with snow and wet mud, and Cathy had to be careful not to fall, but the air rang with bird-song, and squirrels and chipmunks were everywhere. A two-hour walk took her to a fork in the trail where hikers could decide between going all the way to the teahouse or taking an easier, shorter walk, and it was here that Cathy planted her sign in the ground. From this point it was just another twenty minutes or so to the hotel.

She looked around curiously as she went inside, half expecting to see Nicholas, yet knowing he wouldn't be there. It was a lovely place, all glowing wood and warm colours, and a few crackling fires. An ideal place for skiers to return to after a long day on the slopes. Nicholas's pride in his hotel was justified.

The staff at the reception desk were friendly, also a little curious. Evidently they all knew that the teahouse was in new hands, and they'd been wondering when they would meet Cathy. Her appearance seemed to surprise them. Did they know, she wondered wryly, that their employer had spent a few snow-bound days with the girl who'd featured in the notorious assault case? If they did, there was nothing in their demeanour to show it. Would they care? Perhaps not as much as she would have imagined a few weeks ago.

I'm getting over it. The thought came to her suddenly, making her very happy.

It took Cathy at least half an hour to place her orders, and in all that time there was no sign of Nicholas.

'You're going straight back to the teahouse?' asked one of the girls at the desk. 'Why not stay a while?'

'Someone mentioned ski championships . . .'

'That's right. There's a shuttle bus leaving for the slopes in twenty minutes.'

Cathy's smile hid a sudden excitement. 'I think I might go along and watch.'

At the slopes the skiers spilled from the bus, Cathy with them. And then she drew in her breath in excitement.

This must be a fairly major championship, for everywhere there were people. They crowded near the finishing lines and were strung out along the side of the course. A girl was coming down the slope, zigzagging expertly, avoiding obstacles with deceptive ease, her movements fluid and lovely. The excitement of the crowd mounted as she sped along the snow, swelling to a roar as she finished the course. Already the next skier was coming down the slope. In other circumstances Cathy would have watched eagerly, but now her thoughts were elsewhere.

Where was Nicholas?

And then she saw him. His back was to her, and the blue ski-suit he was wearing was unfamiliar to her. Still, she knew it was he. There could be only one man with just that height, that build, that proud bearing. Excitement made a knot in her stomach. She hadn't realised—hadn't let herself realise—quite how much she'd been wanting to see him again.

She was so excited that it was a few moments before she noticed the girls clustered around him. One girl must have said something which caught his attention, for he turned to listen. For the first time Cathy was able to see his profile. He was laughing, and a hand went out to touch the girl's cheek. It was at that moment that the sick feeling hit her. A feeling which was like nothing she had ever felt before, not even in the good days with Lance. All day she'd been wondering how it would be to see Nicholas again. Her mind had been operating on two levels, so that while she'd walked from the teahouse, while she'd placed her orders at the hotel, all the while she'd been thinking of Nicholas. And now she was within yards of him, and she wanted to shove aside the girls who were claiming his attention.

I can't be jealous! she thought incredulously.

This was awful! And the one thing she hadn't anticipated. God, but it had been a mistake to come here! To lay herself open to emotion. Why hadn't she stayed at the cabin? Best to leave now, before Nicholas saw her.

She had taken a few steps in the direction of the shuttle bus when someone called, 'Hey, Cathy.'

It was the hiker, Todd. Only now he was dressed in a ski-suit, and she knew that if he hadn't called to her she would never have noticed him.

'Hi. Glad you decided to come.' He was grinning as he came to her.

'Yes. It's great . . .'

'Did you see Dawn come down the slope a few minutes ago?'

'She was superb.' Cathy's voice was shaking. She must get away.

'The one to watch will be Mary Lucas. She skis in about an hour.'

'I don't think I'll be here by then.'

Todd looked at her disbelievingly. 'Hey, she could be Olympic material.'

'Yes, well, I have to get back.'

'Meet some of the other guys first.' And before she could stop him, he had raised his voice and called, 'Hey, Nick. Here's a neighbour of yours.'

As Nicholas turned Cathy felt her body grow rigid. She wanted only to get away but somehow her brain was refusing to send the correct messages to her limbs.

For a long moment Nicholas seemed as tense as she was. And then he was coming towards her, his hands outstretched. 'Why, Cathy!'

Somehow she forced a smile. 'Hello, Nicholas.' She was shaking, and she didn't want him to know it.

'So you know each other,' she heard Todd say.

'We know each other,' Nicholas confirmed. He was

talking to Todd, but his eyes were on Cathy. He was smiling, the smile she remembered so well. It was as if, without words, he was reminding her of everything that had happened between them.

As if she needed reminding!

For a long moment, as they stood looking at each other, Cathy was oblivious of Todd, of the girls, of all the people on the slope. There was only Nicholas, and she could not have taken her eyes from his face if she'd tried. It was only a few weeks since she had seen him, and yet she felt as if she was seeing him for the first time again.

'How have you been?' he asked softly.

'Just fine.'

'How's the teahouse?'

'I don't think you'd recognise it. I painted all the chairs, Nicholas, and finished wallpapering.'

Such trivial conversation when what she really wanted to say was 'Have you missed me? Have you been thinking of me?' And what she longed to do was touch the tanned face and run her fingers through the tousled fair hair.

'You've been busy,' he said.

'Oh yes.' Had his eyes always been so blue? And had he always been so tall, so athletically built? On these slopes, where well-built men were to be found aplenty, there couldn't be a single one who was as attractive as Nicholas.

'Will you have a muffin for me if I come to visit you?'

Her heart did a funny somersault in her chest. Would he really visit her? 'Coffee too,' she promised.

So quietly that it was impossible for Todd to hear him, Nicholas asked, 'Have you been lonely?'

Oh, how she longed to feel his arms around her! It was a physical thing, this longing. She had never imagined it could feel like this.

'Cathy?' Nicholas prompted.

'A little,' she admitted.

And let him make of that what he wanted. At this moment she was beyond caring what he thought, what he assumed, what construction he placed on her words. She only knew how much she had missed him, and that it would be hell to leave him and go back to the teahouse.

Todd, she saw with relief, had moved aside to talk to the girls who'd been standing with Nicholas. Perhaps he'd grown bored with a conversation which on the surface was so trivial.

'Have I told you that I'm glad you came today?' Nicholas asked.

For the first time it was easy to smile. 'Are you?'

'Very glad. It's another step, Cathy.'

'I guess it is,' she acknowledged.

Something moved inside Nicholas. Cathy was so vulnerable. She tried hard to be cool and self-possessed, and she did not know that in the lovely gamine face her green eyes were haunted.

'I hear the teahouse is beginning to do well,' he said.

She saw the way his gaze went from her eyes to the lips he had kissed, and she thought, neither of us is really saying what we're thinking. She smiled. 'If you call a couple of guests every day or so doing well.'

'Things will pick up once summer comes.'

She was about to say, 'I hope so,' when a girl's voice said, 'Hey, Nicholas,' and another one said, 'Did I hear the word "teahouse"?'

Nicholas stepped aside to include them. 'Anne,

Stephanie—I want you to meet Cathy Lennox, and yes, she's the new owner of the teahouse.'

Anne gave a friendly smile and said, 'Hi,' but Stephanie looked at Cathy curiously. 'Cathy Lennox . . . The name is familiar. Have we met?'

Cathy had never seen the other girl in her life. 'I don't think we have.'

'It will come to me.' Stephanie was frowning. 'I'm so sure . . .' She broke off. Only to say a moment later, 'But of course! Cathy Lennox. The girl in the assault case.'

The smile died in Nicholas's eyes at the same time as Cathy grew rigid.

'You are *the* Cathy Lennox, aren't you? I recognise the face from the photos.'

'Drop it,' Nicholas said.

But the very last thing Stephanie meant to do was to drop the subject.

'I had friends who studied with the man, I forget his name.'

'Stephanie!' Anne said.

'They couldn't believe he did the things you accused him of doing. *Did* you pass the course?'

Cathy clenched her hands tightly in her mittens. 'I really don't think it's any of your business.'

'The case is over,' Nicholas said tersely.

'Of course. I'm just interested.' Stephanie's expression was blandly innocent. 'It's not every day I meet a celebrity.'

'The case is over, I said.' There was steel in Nicholas's voice.

But Stephanie was like a cat that had caught a mouse and was determined to torment it. To Nicholas she said, 'Didn't I hear something about your spending a few days up at the teahouse?'

'We were snow-bound, yes.'

'Snow-bound?' Stephanie laughed. 'Be careful, Nicholas darling, you might find yourself with an assault case on your hands too. The lady could be dangerous.'

Cathy found her voice before either Nicholas or Anne could get a word in. 'At least she's not a prize bitch.'

Stephanie looked furious, and Anne giggled, which made Stephanie even more angry. Nicholas tucked a hand through Cathy's arm.

'Time I got back to the course,' he said. 'Come along.' And when they were out of earshot, 'I'm sorry.'

'Not your fault it happened,' Cathy said lightly.

He looked at her. 'Try to forget it.'

'It's not worth remembering.'

'It certainly isn't. And you *are* a feisty lady.' He gave her arm a quick squeeze before releasing it. 'Look, I've a few things to do. We'll go up to the lodge after that and have some hot chocolate.'

Cathy watched him walk over to a group of skiers who seemed to be waiting for him. A girl showed him a schedule, and Nicholas was all concentration as he studied it. Once she heard his low laugh. Stephanie's rudeness had embarrassed him, but now he had other things to think about.

'You're staying to watch after all?' Todd had come up beside her.

Cathy smiled at him, glad of his company. 'I guess I'll be here a while longer.'

One skier after another made her way down the slopes. And then a girl in scarlet was zigzagging down the course. She was so graceful that she was a joy to watch.

'Lindsay Dunlop,' Todd commented. 'Oh hey, she *is* doing well.'

Lindsay's time was not one of the fastest, but Todd was not the only one who was interested in her progress. A burst of enthusiastic applause greeted her finish. Lindsay must be popular. She was pretty too, Cathy saw, as the girl took off her skis. Her face was small and fragile, and just now it was radiant.

People were calling to her, reaching out to touch her. But she stopped for nobody. She seemed to be making a determined course towards just one person.

Nicholas!

It took a moment for Cathy to understand what was happening, and then the breath stopped in her throat. For Nicholas was going to meet Lindsay, and his arms were outstretched. 'Oh Nick, Nick,' Lindsay cried, and then she jumped into his arms, and her feet left the ground as he hugged her against him. After a moment he put her down then, only to cup her face in his hands as he bent to kiss her.

Cathy watched transfixed. Horrified. She was breathing again, but the breath was painful. She felt ill.

'Wasn't she great!' she heard Todd say, but she couldn't respond. There was only the sick feeling. Earlier, when she'd watched Nicholas with the group of admiring girls, she'd been upset. But what she'd felt then was absolutely nothing to what she felt now. She didn't know how she could bear it.

And suddenly she knew that she did not have to.

Abruptly she turned her back on Nicholas and Lindsay and the others and began to walk away.

A hand touched her arm. She jerked around, thinking it was Nicholas, but it was Todd. 'Cathy?' He was looking at her questioningly. 'Aren't you going to go on watching?'

'No.'

'You said you'd stay.'

'I've changed my mind,' she said harshly.

'Some of the best skiers are still to come.' His expression was puzzled and pleading. 'You'll be sorry if you miss them.'

I'm sorry I didn't miss them all, she thought savagely, but didn't say it because even now, distressed as she was, she knew that she didn't want the words to get back to Nicholas.

At the back of her eyes tears had gathered, and her throat felt choked. She wanted very badly to get away from the slopes, from all the merry crowds, to be alone where she could let the tears fall. She had to shake off Todd, before he saw her distress.

She managed a smile that felt as if it would crack her face. 'I really do have to go, Todd. As it is, I've been away from the teahouse too long.'

She didn't have to wait long for a shuttle bus. When she got to the hotel she didn't go inside but made straight for the trail. At the fork in the path she picked up the sign, and as she walked she kept shoving the end of the stick into the soft ground as if it was some kind of weapon. The tears she had held in check before Todd, and then on the bus, were falling freely now. The wind chilled them on her cheeks, and she stopped her angry stride now and then to dab at them with a mittened hand.

Oh, but she was angry! If Nicholas were to materialise suddenly on the trail she wasn't at all sure that she wouldn't attack him. Men! When you came

down to it they were all the same. Get involved with a
man at your peril, for in the end you were the one who
was hurt. Lance had hurt her in one way, and now
Nicholas had hurt her again in another.

Who was Lindsay? Why had Nicholas never
mentioned her? There had been such emotion in her
face as she'd come to him, such feeling in their
embrace. She had to mean very much to him.

The trail was arduous in parts, and Cathy's
breathing was laboured, but she hardly noticed it. She
could think only of the fragile girl in Nicholas's arms
and try to make some sense of her own feelings.

If only Nicholas had never come to the teahouse. If
only they hadn't been snow-bound. For in the process
something had happened to her emotions, so that the
girl who'd come down the trail this morning—in
search of Nicholas, she might as well face it—was not
the girl Larry had dropped from the helicopter a few
weeks earlier. Something had happened during those
days together in the cabin, and Nicholas had allowed it
to happen. If there was a Lindsay in his life, why in
heck couldn't he have said so?

What was it he'd said to her that last day, when
she'd drawn back from his love-making? 'I'm a normal
man.' Well, he was normal all right. He'd gone from
arms that could not give him all he wanted to arms
that could. The trouble was that with his departure he
seemed to have taken a part of Cathy with him. She
could not forgive him for that.

After more than two hours the teahouse came at last
into sight, nestled in the trees, with mountains rising
behind it. The sun caught the glow of the cedar logs,
and the patio looked bright and inviting. To others
only.

As Cathy went inside her chest was heavy with pain, and she knew that the cabin which had been her haven such a short time ago was a haven no longer. There could be no haven for her while she was near to Nicholas.

CHAPTER NINE

CATHY was sweeping pine needles off the patio on
Monday morning when she caught a glimpse of
movement through the trees at the head of the trail. It
was very early for a hiker to arrive, she thought with
surprise. Though perhaps he had been backpacking,
had spent a cold night in a sleeping-bag out of doors,
and was looking for a hot breakfast.

She kept an eye on the trail as she went on
sweeping. Then the hiker emerged through the trees,
and it was Nicholas.

In a second Cathy had tensed. Her inclination was
to go inside and lock the door and refuse to talk to
him. But of course she couldn't do that, and the fact
that it would be childish was only one of the reasons.

God, but he had a nerve coming up here! Just as if
nothing had happened.

She stopped sweeping as he came nearer, but she
made no effort to go and meet him. Instead she stood
still and watched him approach. Outwardly she looked
calm enough, but inside her every nerve was quivering.
Why was he here?

She didn't smile at him. And as he reached the
steps of the patio she saw that he wasn't smiling
either. If anything, his expression was one of
exasperation.

'Hello, Cathy.'

'Hello, Nicholas.' Her voice was cool. 'Isn't this a
little early to be out for your morning walk?'

The look of exasperation deepened. 'Haven't we got beyond sarcasm? You must have been expecting me.'

She hid the little shiver of nervousness. 'No.'

'You ran out on our date on Saturday.'

I don't believe this, she thought. 'Date?'

'We were going to have hot chocolate together at the lodge, remember?'

She'd spent the last two nights remembering so many things, but hot chocolate hadn't been one of them. Nicholas had the look of an impatient man. As if he had a right to be impatient. Play it cool, she told herself.

She smiled. 'So we were. And now you've come to have hot chocolate here instead. Will coffee do?'

A hand shot out and seized one of her wrists in a hard grip. 'Stop this, Cathy!'

Her skin burned beneath his fingers, and within moments her pulse was beating erratically. Did he feel it? He knew her so well, he could hardly be unaware of the way he affected her.

'Let go,' she ordered.

The long fingers loosened their hold. As Nicholas dropped her wrist Cathy was aware of a familiar sensation. Despite all reason she wanted him to touch her. Am I a little crazy? she wondered bleakly.

Nicholas's eyes were on her, and she saw both a frown and a question. 'Why do I get a feeling that we're back to square one?'

She decided to counter the question with one of her own. 'Why are you here, Nicholas? I can't believe you just felt like a walk this time of the morning.'

'You know damn well why I'm here. Why did you run off like that?'

It was hard to retain her composure. 'I . . . I had to get back to the teahouse.'

'You had a sign up saying the place was closed.'

So he knew about that. 'There were things I had to do.'

'Excuses. Always excuses. Why don't you just admit that you were running away again?'

He really did have a nerve. Well, she was not going to admit how seeing him with Lindsay had upset her.

'I had nothing to run from.'

He made an impatient sound. 'I'm sorry about what happened, I really am. Stephanie's a prize bitch, as you said. I can't add to that.'

She stared at him in amazement. Stephanie was the one person she hadn't thought of when she'd lain sleepless.

'So she recognised your name,' Nicholas went on. 'And others will recognise it too. At least for a while, until someone else becomes news. But most women will be outraged by what happened. It's only the oddballs like Stephanie who will take pleasure in seeing you feel bad.'

'Nicholas . . .'

But he wouldn't let her get a word in. 'You have to stop running, Cathy. You had a bad experience, but you'll get over it. You have to stop being so damn over-sensitive.'

'I'm not over-sensitive,' she protested indignantly.

'No? Then what do you call what you did? A stupid woman makes a tasteless remark, and you retreat like a frightened rabbit. I really thought you had more sense than that.'

His contempt was getting to her. 'I didn't go because of Stephanie,' she said icily.

It was his turn to stare. 'You didn't? Then what was it?'

Too late, she realised that she'd set a trap for herself.

'I . . .I just wanted to go.'

He was frowning. 'There must have been a reason.'

'There doesn't always have to be a reason for everything, Nicholas. I was . . . I was a little bored.'

'You hadn't been at the slopes long enough to be bored. Besides, we were going to the lodge together after . . .'

His words tailed off suddenly And then his expression changed. 'Lindsay Dunlop was skiing.'

Cathy was starting to tremble. Hopefully Nicholas would not notice it.

In a new tone, he said, 'You saw me kissing her.'

Cathy gave what she hoped was an indifferent shrug. 'I don't remember.'

His eyes glittered. 'I think you do.'

'I wouldn't make any difference if I did.'

'It would,' he said smoothly, 'if you were jealous.'

She flinched. 'Don't be ridiculous!'

'Is it ridiculous?'

'Of course it is.' She took a step backwards. 'You really flatter yourself, Nicholas.'

'We'll see if I flatter myself.'

He moved so quickly that she was caught unprepared. In a moment he'd sent the broom flying to the ground as his arms went around her. She saw the descending mouth and felt a familiar panic mixed with anger. She struggled against him, pushing her fists up between his chest and hers, and tried to twist her head away from him, but he managed to kiss her nevertheless. Later, when she was able to think about what had happened, she knew that if Nicholas had been any other man she would have used the defence techniques she had learned—but with Nicholas she forgot them.

His kisses were deep, hungry, searching for the response she refused to give him. She was so angry. It didn't matter that she was on fire, all she knew was that Nicholas was violating her lips, her body. That he had come to her from another woman's arms.

'I hate you!' she hissed when he lifted his head to take breath.

'Good. Hatred is a damn sight better than this cool indifference you've been showing.'

'I can't stand to have you touch me! Don't you understand?'

A hand went to her throat, brushing sensuously over the soft skin, before cupping the back of her head in a huge palm. 'I understand that your body is more honest than your words. You want me, Cathy. And I want you. We both want the same thing.'

'I can't stand to have you touch me when you've just made love to another woman.'

He laughed softly. 'Forget the other woman. There's only one woman on this mountain. One man, one woman.'

He was bending towards her again, and despite everything she wanted him so much, but she managed to say, 'Nicholas, no.'

'Yes, my darling.'

Darling . . . She heard the word, yet tried to ignore it. Darling would be what he would call his Lindsay. Oh, but he was a double-crosser, and she wanted nothing to do with him. It didn't matter that her treacherous body craved his touch—she *knew* that she had to resist him.

He began to kiss her again. She tried to close her mouth against him, but his tongue played around the corners of her lips, teasing, tantalising, till she thought she would go mad. And then, just when she thought she could take no more, he pulled her against him, so she could feel the long hard length of his body against hers. All the playfulness was gone now. His kisses became demanding once more, almost savage, as if he insisted on the response he knew was in her to give. And he was succeeding, for his passion unloosed her control, so that finally she was jerked into a total response. She pressed herself against him as she opened her lips, and her arms went around him.

She heard his sigh of pleasure, then he drew her even closer against him, and she let him, arching blindly towards him, consumed with the need to savour the touch of his body, the hardness of his thighs, the flat muscularity of his chest and belly against her own quivering body.

Time stood still as they kissed and caressed, and got to know each other's bodies all over again. They'd been apart so long—too long—and now it was as if they couldn't get enough of each other. That was the only need, the only reality. Cathy had stopped thinking about Lindsay. In a sense she had stopped thinking at all. There was only Nicholas, and the feelings he stirred up in her, and the thunderous demands of her own body.

So strong were those demands that when he lifted her and carried her inside, she did not resist him. She only said weakly, 'What if someone comes here?'

'Where's a "closed" sign?' he muttered.

She had one, and he put it in the window. Then he came to her again.

He opened the top buttons of her shirt and began to kiss her again, stroking his lips along her throat and her shoulders and the swell of her breasts. And then up again, so that by the time he reached her lips she ached with the longing to make it a mutual kiss. His caresses were so druggingly sensuous that they drowned her panic and her anger. She wanted him never to stop making love to her.

Once, when they drew apart to take breath, she lifted her head to look at him. His face was a little gaunter than she remembered it, but the eyes were still as blue, fringed with long dark lashes, and she thought again how attractive he was. Beside him every other man had to pale in comparison.

'It's been too long,' he said.

'Yes.'

'I shouldn't have stayed away.'

But there was Lindsay. For a moment she was tempted to draw back. Instead she opened the buttons of his shirt as he'd opened hers, and then she pressed herself against him again. Just one man and one woman on the mountain, he'd said. One man, *her* man. And at this moment she was consumed with a primeval need to fight for him.

'Do you know what you're doing to me?' he groaned.

'What?' Her lips nuzzled his chest.

'Driving me out of my mind. That's why I had to come to you.' He slid the shirt from her shoulders, and then his hands were moving over her bare back. 'I haven't been able to sleep some nights because I've wanted you so much.'

'Why did you stay away?'

'You know why. Because you weren't ready.'

He brought a hand forward and cupped a breast, and the breath jerked in her throat as he played with the nipple.

'But you came today.' It was so hard to speak.

'I was so happy when you came to the slopes. I knew I couldn't let you go again. And then when I looked around you were gone. My God, Cathy, if I hadn't had certain duties I would have come after you there and then, and if I'd caught up with you on the trail I'd have put you down on the ground and made love to you there.'

The last words had a certain eroticism which fuelled the fire already raging in Cathy. The sensation in her loins was a kind of pain. Lindsay was forgotten, Lance was forgotten. There was only Nicholas now, and the need, the all-consuming need, to be one with him.

'Love me now,' she whispered.

'Are you really ready?'

'Yes, oh yes!'

'I can't stop this time. Cathy, my darling, you do know that?'

'I don't want you to stop.'

Nicholas groaned. It was a sound filled with pain and pleasure, and Cathy had never heard it before. And then he pulled her to him again, holding her so close that she could feel the strength of his desire against her, even through their clothes.

They undressed each other then, quickly, suddenly greedy with mutual passion. And when they were both unclothed and looking at each other they touched each other, their hands running over curves and angles and textures, worshipping, each getting to know the other again.

'You are so beautiful,' Nicholas said hoarsely.

'You are beautiful too.' She was saying words she had never thought could escape her lips. 'Make love to me, Nicholas.'

Nicholas spread the sleeping-bag on the ground. Then he opened his arms to Cathy, and as she came into them he put her down on the soft bag. He lay down beside her, gathering her to him so that they lay together, feet to feet and hip to hip. Cathy did not know that she was making small sounds of pleasure. Nicholas began to caress her once more, his hands and then his lips on the curve of her stomach, on her thighs, on her breasts. He was terribly excited—she knew it, could feel the evidence of his excitement against her, but still he was intent on giving her pleasure. And he was succeeding. He was arousing her as she had never dreamed she could be aroused. When at last neither of them could bear the suspense a moment longer, he lowered himself on to her parted thighs. There was a moment of sharp pain, but then she was moving with him, gladly, urgently, her pain drowned in the greater ecstasy of fulfilment.

Afterwards they were silent a long time, kissing now and then, touching, but silent. Cathy did not know what Nicholas was thinking. She did know that in all her life she had never felt as replete, as happy, as she did now. She lay with her eyes closed, but conscious of Nicholas beside her. And she knew that she would be happy to lie like this till eternity.

'You're smiling,' Nicholas said at length.

'I guess I am.'

'What are you thinking?'

'That the nightmare's over. I've been frightened for so long, Nicholas.'

'And now you're not frightened any longer?'

She opened her eyes and looked at him, drinking in the strong clean lines of his face and body, revelling in his strength and masculinity. Once it was this masculinity which had scared her—now it gave her joy.

'Not in the same way,' she said. 'Not of you. Though I'll always be cautious where strange men are concerned.'

He trailed his fingers over the satin skin of her stomach. 'I don't want there to be any other men in your life.'

She laughed over the new flame that his touch awakened inside her. 'I was thinking of strangers. Of my hikers.'

'You were never really frightened of them. I always wondered about that.'

'I wanted so much to be up here. I figured that the hikers came with the territory, and that anyone who'd climbed the trail would be so hungry that food would be the only thing on his mind. Besides,' she laughed again, 'you're forgetting my screwdriver.'

'You keep it with you?' he asked curiously.

'It's always within reach. Though I wouldn't use it unless I was really desperate.'

Nicholas was silent again. Cathy wondered what he was thinking.

At length he said, 'You know, we can't go on like this.'

She laughed softly as she nuzzled her lips against his chest. 'Why not? It's rather nice.'

'My meaning exactly.'

'Then what's the problem? The sign is in the window. We can go on as long as we like.'

He laughed too then. 'Wanton creature.'

She cradled her shoulder in his armpit as she turned to look at him. 'Are you saying you don't want to make love to me again?'

'I'm saying I do.' He kissed her, thoroughly, satisfyingly. 'At least once every day.'

Fire licked inside her. 'Greedy, are you?'

'Where you are concerned, yes. That was what I meant when I said we couldn't go on like this.'

'I don't understand.'

'You're too far away from me. Come and live at the hotel.'

'Nicholas—I can't do that.'

'I can't climb the trail every day. It would mean hours away from the hotel.'

She grew very still. 'And I can't be away from the teahouse.'

'I've offered to take it over from you.'

'Yes . . .'

'I'm offering again now.'

'I don't know . . .'

'I want you to be with me.' He turned on his side, gathering her to him. 'I want so much from you. Don't you know that I . . .?'

Something drove her to interrupt him. It was as if she couldn't let herself hear what he had to say. Not yet. 'How would *she* feel about it?'

'She?' Nicholas was puzzled.

'Wouldn't she object if I were on the scene too? Your Lindsay?'

The arms that were holding her loosened. Some of the urgency left the long male body. Cathy had the feeling that he had distanced himself from her.

After a few moments he said, 'Lindsay is just a girl I taught to ski.'

'She seemed more than that. From the way you were both . . . well, she seemed very special to you.'

'She *is* special.' There was a hardness in Nicholas's tone that made Cathy even more tense than before. 'Lindsay was taking part in a championship. She fell, very awkwardly. She was badly hurt. Like me, she thought she would never ski again.'

He was speaking so unemotionally, so coldly. There was a growing coldless inside Cathy.

'Unlike me, she recovered completely. But Lindsay was frightened of going back into competitive skiing.'

'You helped her,' Cathy whispered.

'Yes. Yesterday was the first time she was back on the slopes as a competitor. The kiss you saw was gratitude on Lindsay's part, pride and great happiness on mine.' Deliberately he added, 'No sex involved.'

'Why didn't you tell me?' Cathy asked at last.

'You had only to ask.' He sat up. 'But you wouldn't do that, would you, Cathy? It suited you to think of me as a man who would string two women along with not much respect or regard for either of them. That way you didn't have to commit yourself.'

'That's not true,' she denied painfully, knowing all the while that Nicholas was not far off the mark.

'Isn't it? You took a big step today, Cathy. You let me make love to you.'

'It *was* a big step.'

'Don't think I don't understand that. I do.' He reached for his clothes. 'You've come a long way from the girl who wielded a screwdriver.'

'Well then?' She was trembling.

'You still have to learn to trust.'

'It's not that easy. Don't push me too hard, Nicholas.'

'I know that, darling.' For the first time his voice softened. 'We have time, Cathy. So much time.'

The days grew longer, warmer. Only in places where the sun did not reach was there still snow on Cathy's slope. In the meadow around the teahouse wild flowers were springing up, and the air rang with birdsong. Now and then an elk or a moose would come through the trees, and one morning Cathy discovered, with some trepidation, that a hungry bear had visited the cabin during the night in search of edible garbage.

She was thrilled when the pack-horses came up the trail with fresh supplies. She'd been too long without fresh meat and milk and fruit. Hikers began to arrive more frequently, and Cathy welcomed their coming— the loneliness was beginning to get to her.

Nicholas came when he could, but that was not often. In fact, since the day they'd made love he had visited her only twice. They made love again, and each time it was as exciting as the first time. But he made no further attempt to persuade her to leave the teahouse.

'I'm glad you're not rushing me,' Cathy said once.

They were lying on the sleeping-bag, limbs intertwined, languorous after lovemaking.

'Don't think I don't want to,' Nicholas said gruffly. 'This life we're leading is frustrating all hell out of me.'

Cathy slid her hand over his chest, enjoying the way his muscles tightened beneath her fingers. 'You're a patient man.'

'My patience has limits. But I reckon you'll come to me when you're ready. And now look what you're doing to me, feisty lady. I hope there are no thirsty hikers, because that "closed" sign is going to remain in the window a good while longer.'

Nicholas might not have to wait very much longer, Cathy thought as he began to make love to her again. If there was a part of her that still shied away from giving herself totally to another person, with the trust and commitment this involved, there was another part of her that was beginning to want commitment very much. What did Nicholas have in mind? Marriage or just living together? He hadn't said, and she hadn't asked him. What she did know was that she shared his frustration.

He had never said that he loved her, she thought later, as she watched him wave to her through the trees before heading down the trail. Though he might have been about to once, and she had interrupted him. And that had been because she was not sure of her own feelings. But she was no longer as uncertain as she had been then.

I love him. The realisation came suddenly, hitting her with a kind of shock, and she wondered how long the emotion had been there, in her mind and in her heart, dormant and hidden because she did not want to acknowledge it.

I love him!

She had to tell Nicholas. She ran a little way, calling to him. She could just see his long body far below her, but the trail was winding and a wind was blowing and he did not hear her.

Well, she would tell him the next time he came to see her. Or perhaps she would close the teahouse and go down to the hotel. One way or another she had to tell him. As he'd said, they had so much time. She stared down the trail at the roof of the hotel far in the distance and felt quite dizzy with happiness.

She was in love. Crazily, head-over-heels in love, in a way that she had not thought possible. It was a totally marvellous feeling.

Cathy would have gone to see Nicholas the next day, but the sun was shining and the first hikers arrived early, before she could even give thought to putting the 'closed' sign in the window. Next day she couldn't go either. She understood now what he meant about the problems posed by the distance which separated them. In mind and body she ached with the longing to be with him. She smiled wryly. At last she knew what frustration meant. Nicholas would feel well satisfied if he knew what she was going through now.

The day after that brought a surprise visitor.

She didn't hear the sound of the helicopter as it landed in the meadow beyond the trees. The first she knew of his arrival was when he appeared on the patio.

'Hi, Cathy.'

She turned, saw the familiar weathered face, and ran to him happily. 'Larry!'

'Just dropped off your order.'

'You're not off again right away, surely? Oh, I won't let you go. Not without a cup of coffee.'

'Won't say no to that.' He grinned at her, thinking that if she had been lovely the first time he'd seen her, now she was positively beautiful.

'How do you like it? With milk and sugar?'

'Three spoons,' he said, as he followed her into the kitchen. 'Old man like me needs some sweetening.'

'You're not old,' she protested.

'Not so young either. If I were I'd make a play for

you. As it is . . . You're so radiant, girl, something tells me you've found yourself a man.'

Her cheeks grew warm and she turned away, not wanting him to see in her eyes the answer to his question. She was longing to talk about her new-found discovery, to share with someone the miracle of being in love. And who better than Larry, who had dropped her in the snow in what now seemed another era? But before she could tell anyone, even Larry, she had to tell Nicholas.

'Tell me what you think of my kitchen,' she invited as she poured the coffee and put some muffins on a plate.

'Incredible,' Larry said, sounding awed as he looked around him. 'Absolutely incredible.' He gestured. 'All this stuff new?'

Cathy laughed happily. 'No, it's the things the Mortons left here.'

'You renovated it.'

'Yes.'

He bent to study the detail of a delicate alpine flower. 'You did this art-work?'

'Of course.'

He shook his head. 'You're a genius, girl.'

She laughed again. 'You make me feel good, Larry. Art's my subject, I should be able to paint a flower.'

'A genius,' he repeated.

Larry insisted on carrying the tray to the patio. 'I don't recognise the place,' he said, looking around him. 'The Mortons sure wouldn't recognise it either.'

'You can visit me any time, do you know that? You're doing wonders for my morale.'

'No more than you deserve. Now tell me about this man you've met.'

She shook her head, smiling, resisting the temptation to talk. 'There's nothing to tell. You know how it is up here, Larry. Hikers coming and going all the time.'

Larry buttered a muffin. 'I still say it's no life for a girl. Too darn lonely.'

'Oh, it's not so bad. Look at all the mountains I have for company.'

'Mountains don't keep your bed warm at night.' He grinned at her startled expression. 'I'm old enough to speak my mind without offence.'

And then he asked, 'Have you met Nick Perry?'

It was all Cathy could do to keep the warmth from returning to her cheeks. 'We're neighbours in a manner of speaking.'

'So you are. Good man, Nick.'

'You said that the first day.'

'Told you to make it your business to meet him.'

'I didn't have to. Nicholas was here when I got to the cabin.'

'He was?' It was Larry's turn to look startled. 'Well, how about that for a fast worker.' And giving Cathy no time to wonder what he meant by the words, he went on, 'And what does Nick think of all your improvements to the teahouse?'

'He's impressed.'

'He would be.'

'Actually, he helped me. We ... we were snow-bound those first days, and Nicholas helped me clean the cabin.'

'Well, how about that,' Larry said again. 'Putting up the price for himself.'

Cathy's expression was uncomprehending. 'What do you mean?'

It was Larry's turn to look puzzled. 'You must know that Nick wants the teahouse. Why he's been after the place for years. The Mortons wouldn't let him have it. Some long-standing grudge they had against him, even though he saw to things for them in the winter.'

Cathy heard the words, without really hearing them. Without *wanting* to hear them. 'He could have bought it from them when they decided to retire.'

'They didn't want it to go to him.'

The sun seemed to vanish behind the mountains, and Cathy felt cold. 'He never made a big deal of it,' she said slowly.

'He was here that first day you came, wasn't he?'

'Yes. I thought . . .' She stopped, not knowing what to think. All she knew was that her world had crumbled.

'He must have made you an offer.'

So many offers. And every time Cathy had thought he was willing to take the teahouse off her hands to be helpful, because he disapproved of her living here alone.

'He did offer,' she said slowly.

'And you refused? Strange that,' Larry said reflectively. 'Strong man, Nick Perry. Made a great name for himself as a skier, got rich with the hotel, not used to having anyone say no to him. Yet first the Mortons said no, and then a slip of a girl gives him a hard time. Surprising.'

'Life is full of surprises, you'd think I'd have learned that by now.'

Larry shot her a startled look. 'Oh brother, have I said something I shouldn't have?'

'Not at all.' Cathy's voice was hard. But as she

leaned forwards to take her cup the swing of her hair hid the gloss of tears.

'Cathy? Cathy, is Nick the man who . . .? Oh my God!'

'Some things have to be said, Larry,' she said bitterly. 'Only children can hide from the truth forever.'

CHAPTER TEN

ANGER lent Cathy's feet speed. She didn't notice the scenery as she strode along the trail the next morning. Once she slipped and grazed her knee, but she picked herself up and went on without knowing that she had hurt herself. There was room for only one thought in her mind.

She came to the hotel. Nicholas was nowhere in sight. She walked in, and this time the loveliness of the place made not the slightest impression on her. Today she was receptive to only one emotion, and that was anger. At the reception desk she asked for Nicholas. The girl gave her a startled look. At first she said she didn't know where Nicholas could be found. Then, at Cathy's insistence, she said he might have gone to the boathouse.

It didn't take Cathy long to find him. He was by the shore of the lake, squatting beside an upturned canoe. For just an instant something jerked inside Cathy at the sight of the man who had given her so much happiness. And then she hardened herself. She needed all the strength she could muster. Emotion of a sentimental nature was the one thing she could not afford.

The sand on the path deadened the sound of her footsteps, so Nicholas did not hear her approach. She stood and watched him a few moments, then she said, 'Nicholas,' and he looked up.

'Cathy!' He looked really happy to see her, with a

smile that warmed his eyes.

What an act! she thought bitterly.

'What a wonderful surprise. Do you know, I've been thinking of you all morning.'

'Of me or the teahouse?'

'The teahouse came into it.'

'I bet it did,' she said bitterly.

An eyebrow lifted slightly, as if Nicholas was puzzled by her tone. 'It's a damn sight too far away for my liking. The wretched place keeps us apart.' He put out his arms to her. 'But you're here now, and I haven't even kissed you yet.'

'Nor are you going to.'

His hands had gone to her face while she spoke, cupping it with the tenderness which Cathy loved, so that even now it took her a moment to react. But react she did.

She jerked away from him. 'I don't think you heard me.'

Nicholas looked more puzzled than before. 'Nobody will see us.'

'If I wanted to kiss you it wouldn't matter to me if the whole world was watching.'

'Cathy?' His confusion was giving way to impatience. 'Mind telling me what this is all about? You haven't been yourself from the moment you got here.'

'Oh, I'm myself, Nicholas, believe that I'm myself. This is the Cathy I should have been all along, not the deluded creature who was taken in by a con artist.'

'What the hell are you talking about?'

'The teahouse.'

'The teahouse?' He was disbelieving.

'Yes, the teahouse. Why look so surprised, Nicholas? It's always been the teahouse.'

'You're crazy.'

'On the contrary, I'm more clear-headed than I've been in a long time. You want the teahouse, you've always wanted it. And you thought you'd get it by making me fall in love with you.' She tossed her head at him bitterly. 'Why look so stunned, Nicholas, did you really think I'd never find out?'

A mask seemed to have come over his face. His eyes were bleak, the line of his chin was rigid. 'I think,' he said, 'that we should sit down and talk about this.'

'There's nothing to talk about. You tried to con me. And, do you know, you nearly succeeded.'

The ghost of a smile crossed his lips. 'Did I?' he asked softly.

Tears, treacherous and unbidden, formed behind her eyes. She hated this man. In a way she hated him far more than she'd ever hated Lance, for Lance had not touched her emotions. While Nicholas . . . She had fallen in love with Nicholas. She loved him even now in some strange way that had nothing to do with logic.

'Damn you, Nicholas!' she said suddenly.

'Are we going to talk?'

'I told you, there's nothing to talk about.'

'You've condemned me without giving me a trial.' The smile was gone. 'Okay, Cathy, I'm not about to play stupid. Who told you that I was after the teahouse?'

So he was not going to deny it. An ureasonable little spark of hope was extinguished inside her. 'Larry.'

'And you think that's all I wanted from you.'

'I know it. From the very first day when you were waiting for me to arrive, till now. All the time that you were helping me get over my fear of being touched, when you were making love to me—what you really wanted was a way of acquiring the teahouse that the Mortons wouldn't sell you.'

'I don't believe Larry said all that.' His voice was laced with displeasure.

'He didn't have to. He told me enough. I was able to work out the rest for myself.'

'I thought,' Nicholas said slowly, 'that we talked about trust.'

'Trust!' The word fuelled her anger. She was so furious that it was difficult to keep her voice under control. 'You're a right one to talk to me about trust, Nicholas! You're no different from Lance.'

'That's enough.' Beneath his tan his face had paled, and over his cheek-bones the skin was tight.

'There's a lot more,' she lashed out recklessly.

Without warning he caught hold one of her wrists. His grip was tight, hurting her. Nicholas, who had never hurt her physcally, was hurting her now.

'Let go,' she hissed.

The grip tightened. She could feel every one of his fingers on her skin. She hated it, but at the same time she was aware of an intense excitement. Would there always be this chemistry between Nicholas and herself, she wondered despairingly, so that even when she was most angry with him she could still be stirred by him physically?

'I will not be compared with Lance,' Nicholas said.

'I'll compare you all the same.' She had stopped struggling, for she was scared of giving herself away, and it was important that Nicholas should not know how she was reacting to him even now.

'Lance,' she said, speaking very deliberately, 'tried

to rape me physically, because he wanted my body and I wouldn't give it to him. In your own way you raped me too, Nicholas.'

She heard the angry hiss of breath. 'Stop this, Cathy.'

'Why? Because it hurts to hear the truth?' She threw back her head and gave a humourless laugh. 'You conned your way into my life, Nicholas. You knew how I felt about men, but you seduced me anyway.'

'I didn't seduce you. You were a very willing partner when it came to it.'

'Of course, because by then you'd seduced my senses. I wanted you so much. I overcame my fear because I wanted you so much. And all the time you had only one end in mind. The teahouse. And when I'd given you that—as I might have—what would have happened to me then? Would you have discarded me with the garbage?'

'That's an insulting question. I don't think you need an answer.'

'No,' she agreed. 'I don't. There's really just one thing left to say, Nicholas.'

Blue eyes had hardened to steel. 'What is that?'

'You can have the teahouse.'

She felt the jerk of his fingers on her wrist. She had taken him by surprise, she'd said the very last thing he'd expected to hear.

'I see . . .'

'I'd have thought you'd be more enthusiastic. Don't you want to hear my price?'

'Not particularly.'

She stared at him. 'I'll tell it to you anyhow.' She named the figure, and when he didn't respond she went on. 'It's more than I paid the Mortons, but I've done a lot to the teahouse since I brought it, so it's worth more.'

'I don't want it,' he said.

'I don't understand . . .' For the first time she felt uncertain.

'You don't, do you?' His eyes were hooded, enigmatic. It was almost as if he had the upper hand. And that was ridiculous in the circumstances.

'Are you really saying no?' she asked at length.

'For the moment anyway.'

And what was she to make of that?

'Go back to the teahouse,' Nicholas suggested. 'Do some thinking.'

'I'm not a child, Nicholas.'

'No,' he agreed softly.

He had dropped her hand. Now he reached out and touched her face. The palm of his hand stroked a sensuous path that went from her cheeks to her lips and then down her throat. Cathy forced herself to stand very still. His hand was having an appalling effect on her, and telling herself that she hated him, that she felt absolutely nothing for him, did not seem to help.

'No,' he said again. And then, 'You're not a child.'

She swallowed. 'You used the words "for the moment". Does that mean you *are* interested in buying the teahouse?'

'It means I might be interested, but not today.' He paused, then said. 'You haven't told me why you want to sell. Why now? You were always so sure it was what you wanted.'

'I've changed my mind.' She met his gaze. 'I'm going back to Calgary. I've learned that I can live among people.'

'And that's the only reason?'

Very deliberately she said, 'I can't bear to be anywhere near you.'

The next days passed in a kind of numb blur. Hikers came and went, and Cathy served them muffins and sandwiches and coffee. She listened to their tales of the wildlife they'd seen and the places where they had camped. And none of it meant very much to her.

She had put so much of herself into improving the teahouse, into making it her haven, her own lovely place. And now she was having difficulty thinking of it as a haven at all. She'd spoken no more than the truth when she'd told Nicholas that she was ready to face life amongst people again. The encounter with the vicious Stephanie had shown her that she could handle herself. She understood now that the teahouse had never been more than a bolt-hole for her, a place where she could come to terms with what had happened. She would miss it, but she was missing being with people. She needed to be with people, she needed a more permanent companionship than the hikers could provide. The loneliness was getting to her. But it was a problem which could be solved easily enough—she had only to sell the teahouse.

It was the other problem which made her so unhappy, and that one was harder to solve. Wherever she looked, wherever she went, whatever she did, there were memories of Nicholas. At night she dreamed about him. Leaving the mountains and going back to Calgary would not help her with that. She could travel the world and Nicholas would still be with her. Short of ripping out her heart and mind and soul she would never be rid of him. He was part of her now.

Over and over she asked herself the same question—why was it so difficult to forget a man she hated?

There were other questions as well. Nicholas should have jumped at the offer of the teahouse. Why had he not done so? He'd said, 'I might be interested. But not now, not today.'

Why the hesitation? Cathy wondered.

She kept wondering when he would come up the trail to discuss the sale with her. Whenever she saw a tall man through the trees there were a few moments when she thought it might be Nicholas. Each time her heart pounded and the palms of her hands grew damp. But Nicholas never came.

Finally she'd had enough of living in limbo. It was time to make another approach. Only this time she would not go to see Nicholas. So she wrote him a letter, renewing her offer, inviting him to negotiate. She gave the letter to a hiker who was a guest at the hotel, and asked him to deliver it for her.

She did not have to wait long for a reply. It came the next day. Delivered by another hiker.

When Cathy had finished serving the hiker she went into the kitchen and tore open the envelope. The note was short and impersonal, though not unfriendly. 'I don't negotiate by correspondence. However, your offer is interesting. Come and see me and we can talk about it.' It was signed simply, 'Nicholas'.

Not 'love, Nicholas'. Not 'affectionately'. Well really, she asked herself crossly, what had she expected?

So the ball was back in her court. He was an

interested buyer, but he was not eager. Unless this was just one more game he was playing. Come and see me. Some nerve he had! Her reaction was to tell him what he could do with his suggestion. But she wanted to sell. And Nicholas was not turning out the enthusiastic buyer she'd imagined. It seemed that much as she dreaded the idea of having to see him, if she wanted to sell she would just have to ignore her pride and do as he asked.

She waited until Monday, which was generally a slow day at the teahouse. She went down the trail, planted her sign at the fork where she'd put it the first time, and then walked on towards the hotel.

At the lake she stopped. The water was a deep translucent turquoise now, so calm and clear that the snow-covered peaks of the surrounding mountains were an unbroken reflection on its surface. But Cathy had no eye for the beauty all around her. She could only think of Nicholas, of their meeting. She'd been feeling nervous all the way down the trail, and so she stood at the shore of the lake and took a few deep steady breaths to give herself courage and strength. Nicholas could do no more than say no. And if that was his answer, well then her next step would be to advertise. It was really quite simple. It was only her foolishly fevered state of mind that was making her see difficulties which did not exist.

Stay cool, she reminded herself. Cool, calm, unemotional.

None of which was going to be very easy. She knew that the moment she saw him. He was in the hotel lobby, his eyes on a sheaf of papers in his hand. She saw him before he saw her, and for a long moment she stood quite still, curling her fingers tightly in the palms of her hands, hating herself for the way her stomach had turned into a hard knot of tension.

Her mouth was very dry, but she managed to say, 'Hello, Nicholas.'

At the sound of her voice he turned. She caught an expression in his eyes that she had never seen there before, but it was gone so quickly that a moment later she was wondering if she had imagined it. And then he was coming towards her.

'Why, Cathy.'

She took a step away from him. 'I've come to talk to you.' Curt, formal, crisp. Let Nicholas be under no illusion as to the reason for her visit—she was a woman who wanted to make a deal.

His eyes gleamed. 'Fine. We'll go to my cabin, we can talk there.'

'No.' She took another step backwards. 'We can talk here.'

'In my cabin,' Nicholas said over her protest. He turned to the girl at the desk. 'Phyllis, please see that I'm not disturbed.'

He walked away from the desk then, and Cathy had no option but to follow. If her stomach had been tight before, now it was a hard knot of pain. The idea of being alone with Nicholas frightened her. It was also terribly exciting. That was what shocked her the most. She did not want to be excited by Nicholas, not now, when this was probably the last time she would ever see him.

Appallingly, that was the thought which was uppermost in her mind. She should have been thinking about the sale, about a purchase price and an occupation date, and all she could think about was that after today she would never see Nicholas again.

'You always have to have your way,' she said irritably, to hide her torment.

He only smiled at here. 'Come along, Cathy.'

His cabin was next to the main building. Nicholas opened the door and Cathy followed him inside. But she refused to look around her. She had enough memories to burden her, she did not want any more.

'Let's talk,' she said.

'Sit down, Cathy.'

She remained standing. 'About the teahouse . . .'

'Please sit,' he said. 'Might as well be civilised.'

Civilised! There was nothing civilised about the way she felt about him, wanting to be in his arms, wanting to hurt him, all at the same time. He was very close to her, towering over her, making her feel vulnerable. She did not want to feel vulnerable, and so she sat down on the nearest chair. He pulled up a chair just a foot or so away.

If only he wasn't so attractive. Even now, when all reason warned her to resist him, there was a magnetism that evoked a primitive response in Cathy. She drew a breath. 'Last time we talked you said you might be interested in buying the teahouse.'

'I remember.'

'Have you thought any more about it?'

Nicholas's eyes were on her face, lingering on her lips. 'I didn't have to. My thoughts have always been clear on the matter.'

'You really are an arrogant bastard.'

'And you,' Nicholas said, 'are still a feisty lady.'

She wished he hadn't said that. Feisty lady. It had the ring of an endearment. It had been their own special phrase, it evoked all those memories she wanted so much to forget.

She kept her voice as business-like as she could. 'If your thoughts were so clear, why, when I came to talk to you, did you send me away?'

'Because in the mood you were in you would have said no to my terms.'

Cathy wasn't sure why she shivered. 'I might say no now.'

Very softly, Nicholas said, 'I hope you won't.'

At the lake she had resolved to be cool and calm and unemotional, but that was hard when Nicholas, crafty rogue that he was, seemed to have taken control of the situation. He knows I'm nervous, she thought.

With a crispness she was far from feeling, she asked, 'Well, Nicholas, do you want it or don't you?'

'Very much.'

He was making her angry. 'Why couldn't you have just told me so in your letter? Why did you ask me to come here?'

'I think you know the answer to that.'

'The price is too high?'

'Actually, I haven't given the price a thought.' His tone was lazy but the eyes that studied her were intent.

She was finding it hard to control her trembling. 'What is it then?' And when he didn't answer, 'What else is there to discuss?'

'My terms.'

'*Your* terms?'

'Right.'

He was playing with her, and the gleam in his eyes showed he was enjoying every moment of it. She didn't want to ask the question because she didn't want to hear the answer. But finally she had to ask it. 'Okay then, what are your terms, Nicholas?'

'You come with the teahouse.'

She stared at him, stunned. 'You mean . . . you want me to run it for you? You don't understand, Nicholas, I have to get away.'

'I want,' he said very softly, 'you to be my wife.'

This wasn't happening. It couldn't be.

Over an unreasoning explosion of happiness, Cathy said, 'You don't know what you're saying.'

Nicholas was smiling, but across his high cheek-bones the skin was taut. 'My thoughts have never been clearer.'

'Nicholas . . . Nicholas, you're crazy!'

Something moved in his face. 'You've certainly done your very best to drive me out of my mind.'

She put her hands over her eyes. She had come down the mountain today ready to do battle with Nicholas, and with just a few words he had turned her world upside down. Inside her happiness was waging war with confusion, so that she didn't know what to think.

At last she looked up. 'I don't know what to say. Nicholas, you said your terms . . . were those really your terms when I came to see you the first time?'

His gaze was steady. 'They've been my terms since the first day we met. You don't believe that, do you?'

She shook her head, unable to take it all in. 'But Larry said . . .'

'Larry told you I wanted the teahouse, and he was right. I came up that first day to welcome you. I also offered to buy the teahouse. But you've known that all along.' His face was hard now.

'Yes . . .' Mixed with the happiness there was also the sense that something was wrong. 'Why are you so angry, Nicholas?'

'Because I wonder when you're going to stop

running. You ran because you thought I was having an affair with Lindsay. And then you ran again because you thought all I was after was the damned teahouse. When are you going to stop, Cathy?'

For once she didn't have to think about the answer. It came to her naturally, quite on its own. And she knew, as clearly as she had ever known anything in her life, that it was the right answer. 'I've stopped running, Nicholas.'

'Do you mean that, Cathy?' His tone was suddenly urgent.

'Yes.' Her heart was in her eyes. She loved this man, she had loved him for ever, so it seemed. She would never run away from him again.

He leaned forwards and took her hand in his. His palm lay flat against hers, and then his fingers closed over her hand. Cathy felt happier than she had been in a long time. This was how it should be—the small hand in the big one. But she wanted more from Nicholas now, so much more.

'All I want is to make love to you,' Nicholas said hoarsely, 'but there are things that have to be said. I did want the teahouse. The Mortons wouldn't sell it to me, and I thought I would buy it from you. But then . . . You walked in out of the snow with your screwdriver, and things changed. You were so feisty and yet so vulnerable. You saw the dreadful rooms, but your spirit never faltered. I fell in love with you.'

Cathy didn't want to say it, but she had to. 'But you still wanted the teahouse.'

'Only because I wanted to get you out of there. The teahouse wasn't important any more.'

'And now?' She was so happy that she thought she would burst with the intensity of her emotion.

'You'll have to get someone to run it for you.'

'For us,' Cathy said.

He stood up, pulling her with him. 'Does that mean you'll marry me?'

'Yes, oh yes, Nicholas.'

'I love you, feisty lady. You're in my blood, you're part of me. I was so scared I'd lost you.'

'You could never do that, because I love you too. I think I did almost from the beginning. I was just so frightened . . . after Lance . . . that I didn't let myself know it.'

He was so close to her that she could feel every inch of his long body. All she wanted now was to make love with him.

Nicholas said, 'Will you be able to trust me now?'

'Yes.'

'Do you know I would never hurt you?'

'I've always known that, I think.'

He cupped her face with his hands. 'For everything that puzzles you there will always be an answer. There has to be, because I love you.'

'And I love you.' She wound her arms around his neck, pressing herself to him. 'Did I hear you give orders not to be disturbed?'

She could feel the laughter in his throat. 'Yes.'

'Then can we stop talking and make love?'

'Yes, my darling, we can.' He began to kiss her, hungrily, tantalisingly, awakening her as only he could. In the moment before he led her to the bedroom he looked down at her. 'My darling Cathy,' his voice was husky now, 'I want to make love to you to the end of time.'

Her secret from the past unlocked the door to her future.

In the Venice of 1819, the Contessa Allegra di Rienzi gave her love to the scandalous poet Lord Byron and left the legacy of a daughter he would never know.

Over 100 years later Allegra Brent discovered the secret of her ancestors and travelled to Venice in search of di Rienzi's heirs. There she met the bloodstirring Conte Renaldo di Rienzi and relived the passionate romance that started so long before.

W⬤RLDWIDE

LEGACY OF PASSION.
Another longer romance for your enjoyment.
AVAILABLE FROM SEPTEMBER 1986. PRICE £2.95.

Merry Christmas one and all.

CHANCES ARE
Barbara Delinsky

ONE ON ONE
Jenna Lee Joyce

AN IMPRACTICAL PASSION
Vicki Lewis Thompson

A WEEK FROM FRIDAY
Georgia Bockoven

THE GIFT OF HAPPINESS
Amanda Carpenter

HAWK'S PREY
Carole Mortimer

TWO WEEKS TO REMEMBER
Betty Neels

YESTERDAY'S MIRROR
Sophie Weston

More choice for the Christmas stocking. Two special reading packs from Mills & Boon. Adding more than a touch of romance to the festive season.

AVAILABLE: OCTOBER, 1986   PACK PRICE: £4.80